To Dream of You

THE ROYAL HOUSE OF ATHARIA

TAMARA Gill

COPYRIGHT

To Dream Of You
The Royal House of Atharia, Book 1
Copyright © 2020 by Tamara Gill
Cover Art by Wicked Smart Designs
& Chris Cocozza Illustration
Editor Grace Bradley Editing
All rights reserved.

ISBN: 978-0-6489312-1-8

DEDICATION

For the wonderful ladies in the Historical Hellions reader group. This one is for you. xx

CHAPTER 1

Sotherton Estate, Suffolk, 1805

My Lord Balhannah,
Drew…
*I write to you today from necessity and desperation, and I hope you
shall heed my words and help me due to our friendship. There is no
doubt in my mind that in the coming days your father shall demand
that our marriage takes place forthwith. In fact, as I write this, my
father is readying the coaches to travel two days hence. I assume a
marriage license has already been procured and contracts signed, unbe-
known to us of course…until today.*
*Know that as much as I admire and care for you as a friend, I do not
love, nor do I wish to marry you, as I'm sure you do not want to
marry me. You see, my heart has long been given elsewhere, and I will
not, not even on pain of disinheritance, give up the man I love.*
*When we arrive at Sotherton, please do not be there, unless you wish
to break my heart and give yourself to me before God, when you know
that I shall never love you how a wife should love a husband. If you
can provide me with time, my love has promised to come and collect
me at Sotherton, where we shall run away to Scotland and be*

1

married. I'm sorry to be so frank with my words, but I'm desperate to get this letter to you and, with it, stress how much I do not want such a union.

Please do whatever you can to dissuade this marriage from going ahead.

Forever your friend,

Myrtle

*D*rew placed the missive from Myrtle into the fire in his room and went to the window. He pulled back the heavy brocade velvet curtains to gauge the weather. A perfect spring day, and from his window, he could see the sea and the cove where his small sailing raft was kept.

Absently he listened to his valet, Jeffries behind him go about his duties in his room. He could not stay here. Not with Myrtle so heartsick over their impending marriage. With his decision made, he turned and faced his servant. "I'm going sailing and may even travel down the coast to visit Sir Percival's at Castle Clair in Kent. I will meet you there. Please pack me a small bag to get me through until we meet again. Nothing too fancy, mind you, we'll be mostly hunting or taking our leisure about the estate. Maybe only two dinner jackets."

Jeffries stared at him, his eyes wide with this change of plans. Drew raised one brow, waiting for him to comprehend he was serious with his demand.

"Of course, my lord." Jeffries started for the chest of drawers, pulling out cravats and buckskin breeches before walking into Drew's dressing room to collect a trunk. "Will His Grace be aware of your travels, my lord, or are we keeping this excursion a secret?" Jeffries asked, from the small room.

Drew went to his chest of drawers and pulled out the oldest buckskin breeches he owned. He stripped his perfectly tied cravat from his throat, along with his waist-coat. Rummaging through his cupboard, he couldn't find his old woolen waistcoat that was warm and what he liked to use for sailing. "I cannot locate my…" Drew smiled when Jeffries passed it to him, a small smile on the man's face. "Thank you," he said, slipping it on, along with his coat.

Drew walked over to his desk and scribbled a short note to his father. Folding it, he handed it to his manservant. "Have this sent from London when you move through there. The duke may travel to town and demand answers, he will try to find me, but he will not succeed. Under no circumstances are you to tell him where I've gone. I will send a word in a week notifying you, God willing, of my safe arrival." His father was ruthless when it came to having his way, the marriage to Myrtle no different. He would lose his allowance, Drew had little doubt, but what of it? It would not be forever. Myrtle would run away and marry, and then Drew could return home.

Thank heavens Miss Landers was also against the union and only needed time to ensure their marriage would never happen. And time is what he was buying now.

Jeffries handed him a small black valise. "Yes, my lord."

Drew pocketed some blunt and left, leaving via the servant's stairs and the back door, two places his father's shadow never darkened. He ran a hand through his short locks, pulling on a cap to disguise himself further.

The brisk, salty tang of sea air hit him and invigorated his stride. Drew walked through the abundance of gardens his mother had so painstakingly cared for before passing last year. Memories of running about the garden bombarded his mind. Of hidden vistas and large oaks that any young boy enjoyed frolicking around whenever he could. His mother had designed the garden to incorporate hidden vistas perfect for children. Plants that camouflaged the old Roman ruins on the south side of the park, so it wasn't until you were almost upon them did the ruins reveal themselves, the long-lost castle of the Sotherton dukes who came before them.

Drew had spent hours playing on his own within the walls of this green sanctuary. As much as he disliked having the idea of a wife at this very moment, he couldn't help but look forward to the day his children would run about the beautiful grounds and enjoy what he always had.

The crashing of the waves echoed through the trees. Stepping free of the manicured grounds, Drew stood at the top of the small cliff and looked down on the beach's golden sands below. Many years ago, he'd had a small boathouse built to house his sailboat, and as the tide was high, it would be no problem pulling it out and dragging it the short distance to the water.

Taking the winding path down to the shore, it didn't take him long to haul the boat into the shallows and throw his bag under the little compartment that would keep it dry. The sky remained clear, with only the slightest sea breeze. It would help him travel down the coast to where his friend and closest confidant Sir Percival lived. The trip should only take a few days, and he couldn't get far enough away from this estate. To be forced into a union, not of his choice, or Miss Lander's, was reprehensible. The year was 1805, for heaven's sake. His father really ought to get up with the times. Step into the nineteenth century and embrace the new era. He was a grown gentleman, fully capable of making his own decisions. For his father to demand he marry, simply because he'd stumbled across an heiress, was offensive.

Drew pushed off from the shore, releasing the sail. The wind caught the sheet and pulled him out to sea at a clipping pace. He steered south and smiled. His father would forgive him in time, he was sure of it. The duke was never one to hold a grudge for long, and no matter how mad he'd be at finding out Drew left, he would get over it in time.

CHAPTER 2

*H*olly Devereux galloped hard down the shore that sat adjacent to her secluded estate. The wind whipped at her hair, and it fell about her shoulders, her village hat slipping behind her head and hanging on only by the blue ribbon about her neck.

Her mount, a trusty gray stallion, thudded down the beach, whipping up the sand and sea to slap at her breeches, making them sodden. Her boots would take some days to dry out after this outing. But it was so worth it.

She pushed him on, laughing at the speed with which she traveled. How wonderful to be so free, to enjoy life as everyone should, with basic needs met and love of nothing else but yourself and your pets. So different to her life back in Atharia. How she would live when she became queen.

Only a few more weeks, and she would be old enough to rule, and her uncle would have to step aside.

Even so, life before now seemed foreign and unknown, part of another time, another woman's story. Not hers at all.

Holly spotted something on the beach, and she slowed her mount. Was it driftwood lying where the surf broke against the sand? She reined in her horse to a walk, trying to make it out. She jumped down, running when she realized the lump of wood wasn't that at all, but a man.

Her heart thumped hard in her chest as she raced toward him, her steps hindered by the sand's depth and the surf that made her boots waterlogged.

Thinking of her uncle and his attempt on her life in London, she pulled out the small pen knife from the leather sheath that sat in her boot. Was this man a trap? Someone sent by her uncle to lie in wait before striking at her when no one else was about? She stood on the shore for a time, debating what to do. The surf crashed over him, but thankfully he was lying face up and not the other way around. Was he alive? She could not tell from this distance, and she fought with herself whether she wanted to find out.

What if this was a trap? Her uncle had certainly become shrewder in ways to strike at her when she was most vulnerable. Holly looked about again, and seeing no one else around, decided to do the right thing and help. She would either be damned or a savior.

Holly kneeled beside the motionless fellow and placed her ear to his chest. Nothing, no beat or rise of his chest with each breath. Standing, she pulled him away from the shore up to where the sand was dry. He was heavy and wet, which made it doubly hard, but she managed it with all her might. Holly opened his waistcoat and, pulling his shirt down, listened again. A faint but slow thump sounded soft, but was there, and she sighed, relieved to hear he was alive, although not by much.

Living as remote as she did, there was no point in

shouting for help. Her guards who acted as her servants were too far away, and with the wind as fierce as it was, her words would only be carried away out over the ocean. Holly touched his chiseled cheek, gasping at the chill of his skin. She needed to get him warm, and fast. Not certain why he was here, she searched his pockets and breeches for any weapons, thankfully finding nothing but a hand-kerchief.

"Damn you," she said, standing once again and drag-ging him into the sand dunes. Her horse snickered and followed. She would have to warm him with her own body. He was as still as someone who'd passed away, and the blue on his lips proved that had she not come across him when she had, the man's life would've been over by nightfall.

Taking a deep breath, she lay on top of him, pulling his chest against hers. A gasp escaped at the shock of feeling his chilled skin against her warmth.

Holly shivered, but soon warmth replaced the cold between them, his heart beat harder against her ribs. With the immediate danger of him dying dispelled, Holly inspected his features. His cutting jaw was shaded with a little stubble, the hair on his head was short, but still long enough for one to run their fingers through it if they wished. He had a straight, sharp nose, which was probably a good thing. No one could be perfect. Otherwise, there wasn't much wrong with him. The stranger was perfectly proportioned, even his body beneath hers was hard and muscular, if not resembling an ice brick at present. No pockmarks marred his skin, nor did he seem in need of sustenance. A well-looked-after stranger, that was certain.

Holly lay her head in the crook of his neck and hugged him closer, letting her mind wander in thought. Where had the man come from? She'd seen no boat, so he was either lost, or some accident had befallen him. Of course, a worse thought was that he was one of her uncle's henchmen sent to find out her location that would eventuate in her death. In which case, saving him now would be one of the worst mistakes she'd ever made.

They would need to find out who he was and why he was here. It was paramount to her safety. Her uncle was a ruthless man, a trait that was only newly realized after the king, her father, had passed away. He would stop at nothing to keep the Atharia crown from falling onto her head.

She couldn't determine how long she lay there, but in time, warmth started to replace the cooled skin of his body, and he started to make sounds of a man coming out of unconsciousness. Reaching up, she patted his cheeks. Slapping him a little harder than she meant when he didn't respond. "Sir? Wake up. Sir?"

His eyes fluttered open, and she stared into the deepest blue orbs she'd ever seen. He mumbled something incoherent, and she patted his cheek to keep him with her. "Wake up, sir. You're safe."

Holly disentangled herself from him, only to turn and find him staring at her with ill-concealed shock.

Heat bloomed on her cheeks, and ignoring his reaction to her laying on him, she stood. "Are you well, sir? How do you feel?"

He struggled to sit up, then collapsed back onto the sand. Holly frowned, hoping he wasn't too ill. She needed to get them both away from the shore before nightfall. Exposure to the elements would not help the gentleman to get better. She looked about again, hoping he was as alone as he seemed.

"My head. It's pounding."

His voice was English, and a deep rumble and hoarse, probably from lack of water. Holly whistled for her horse. Her gray stallion lifted its head from a grassy patch on the dunes, snickered, and trotted over to her. Holly took out the small water bag she always carried with her and handed it to him. "Drink this. It'll help you feel better."

The man took a small sip and coughed before taking a good, hearty swallow. "Thank you," he rasped. "I think I owe you my life."

Holly shook her head, no thanks required. "I only did what anyone would do when finding another human being on the beach, half-dead." She paused. "Do you think you can stand and make it to my horse? I really need to get you out of this weather. Another storm is brewing in the west and will blow through here tonight."

He rubbed his forehead, lines marring his brow. "There was a storm last night, yes?"

"A terrible one," Holly agreed. As it was, some of her guards who worked in the stable were busy fixing the roof of the barn. Two windows at the rear of the house had blown out with the force of the wind. Not to mention around Lord Bainbridge's estate, there were trees and limbs down all over the property. It would take weeks for all of it to be cleared and back to normal.

She helped him to stand. "Who are you, sir?"

He stared at her a moment, and panic flickered in his eyes. "I have no idea," he said at length, stumbling toward her horse when he went toward it. "My leg." He reached down, and Holly noticed the red pool of blood on his trousers.

"You're injured." She took out her knife again and cut the material away from the wound. "It's a cut, but I do not believe it is deep enough for stitching. We will tend the wound when we return to the estate." Holly caught him around the waist and helped him over to her mount.

"You do not know your name or where you came from?" His skin pallor told Holly he was unwell, and perhaps with a good night's sleep, food and water, his memory lapse would wane. "Here, climb up on the horse, and we'll travel back to where I'm staying. You may sleep in the stables, and I'll have one of the servants tend to you until you are better."

He nodded but didn't say anything as he scrambled onto the horse's back. Holly mounted behind him and urged her horse for home. It was only two miles to her small estate, and it would not take them long since the wind was blowing behind them, pushing them inland.

They cleared the dunes and traveled for some time in quiet. The man huddled into his torn jacket and damp clothing. Holly hoped he didn't catch the ague after she'd managed to keep him from dying thus far.

By the time they arrived back at the estate, he was slumped over her horse's neck and threatening to fall off. Holly yelled out for Niccolo, her most senior guard, who took care of the estate's security. He ran from around the back of the stables and was there to help before the stranger dropped to the ground.

"Oh, my word, Miss Holly. What have you found here?"

"Help me, Niccolo. He's about to fall off."

Niccolo maneuvered the man onto his wide, strong shoulder and walked backward, slipping the unconscious gentleman off the horse. Holly jumped down, handing her mount to Lorenzo, her head stableman and second in charge. "I found him on the beach, almost dead. I'm not sure if he washed up, was dumped, or is one of my uncle's henchmen. He also has a wound on his leg that you'll have to have Mario clean. He is in a frightful mess, and I'm concerned for his welfare, but more importantly, we need to find out who he is and until then, keep a watch on him at all times."

Niccolo shouted out orders for the stable staff to light the fire in the men's quarters and place a cot close to the hearth. Holly followed him to the room and stood back as the men went about Niccolo's orders. When they went to strip off his shirt, her head guard paused, raising one brow in her direction. "It's probably best, Miss Holly if you wait outside and let us take over from herein. We'll give the man a shot of brandy, and if you could have cook bring out a bed warmer, that'll be right good."

Holly nodded. "Of course. I'll go and tell her straight-away, and let me know if there's anything I can do. I'll be in the library if you're looking for me."

Niccolo tipped his head. "Right you are, Miss Holly," he said, pulling the shirt fully from the man. Holly took a calming breath at the sight of his naked chest. So firm and strong, lovely tanned color and smooth. In her haste to warm him, she had not had the time to admire his athletic build, but she could now. The man, no matter who he was, was akin to an Adonis.

She hoped the heat burning her cheeks wasn't notice-able to her men whom she passed on her way to the house. A princess did not blush over the body of a common man. How vulgar.

Even so, she had to admit the stranger was as hand-some as sin. And if Holly knew anything at all, it was that sin was not to be sought. Her marriage would be to a man of royal blood or connections—a man who brought wealth and power so no one could threaten Atharia or her people again.

Once she removed her uncle from the throne that he had stolen from her.

The kitchen's warmth was a welcome reprieve from the chilling wind that had accompanied the storm the night before as she stepped inside. Cook looked up from rolling dough on the table and smiled. "Miss Holly, lovely to see you today. Is there something I can help you with?"

"Can you send out a heating pan to the staff quarters? I found a man today on the beach, and he's quite cold and in need of warming up. Actually, make it two pans. He may need more than one. He was in a frightful state." Holly started for the library. "I shall have tea and biscuits in Lord Bainbridge's office if you please."

For a moment, Holly watched the cook pack the warming pan with red-hot coals from the stove and prepare a small meal for the stranger. It must have been the man's lucky day, for had her mount not needed a run after missing yesterday due to the storm, she would never have gone, and his fate could've been quite different.

The cook placed the food onto a tray for a maid to take out to the stable. "Do you believe he's going to survive? What a terrible situation for you to come across, not to mention an unfortunate situation for the man as well."

Holly could not agree more. The circumstances were quite shocking. "With rest and the warming pans, I'm sure he'll pull through. If we heat him from the inside as well as out as we intend, I'm sure he'll recover. He certainly looks stern enough."

Niccolo poked his head into the kitchen and stepped inside when he spied her. "I've come to collect the pans, but I wanted to confirm that we'll tell the lad once he's coherent the same as we tell everyone else we've encountered."

"Yes, I think that's best since we do not know who he is or if he's working for my uncle," Holly said, putting a small teacup on her tray.

"I will have two men follow him at all times. Of course, with his wound, he'll not be going far for a day or two. Even so, once he's healed, we shall shadow him, and he'll be none the wiser." Niccolo stood tall and clasped his hands behind his back while waiting for a reply.

Holly was pleased with her guard's unfailing support and care. "I'm only two months away from returning home to Atharia to take up my duties there. The man doesn't need to know anything other than I'm Miss Holly Devereux visiting from abroad. If he is not one of my uncle's men, being here puts him in danger, and unfortunately he'll be held here while he recovers. We need to keep watch of him at all times and never allow him to be near my person without one of the guards attending with him."

"Of course, Miss Holly."

Niccolo bowed deeply, backing out of the kitchen, hands full with warming trays, a maid following close on his heels with the stranger's food.

Holly watched as the cook placed a steaming pot of tea on her tray, the biscuits and teacup already set upon it. "I can carry this to the library. Thank you, Mrs. Colton." Holly ignored the servant's protests, carrying the tray herself. The last three months in England had been the most delightful she'd ever known, up to the point her uncle had tried to take her life. Now it was a waiting game, a time to remain hidden in the English countryside before she could return home and face her tyrant uncle.

Holly wasn't afraid to admit that she would miss England when she returned home. The land, the solitude where she could hear herself think, had given her time to see another way to live. She was a stronger woman now, and she would need to be strong for what awaited her back in Atharia. Her uncle would not be an easy man to overthrow.

A knock on the door sounded before Mrs. Colton entered and curtsied. "Miss Holly, the man you found on the beach today has woken. A promising sign, to be sure. He was curious as to who found him. He doesn't seem to know where he is."

"Thank you." Holly stood and went to the windows that looked out over the estate's western side. The sun was dipping in the west, and dusk was upon them. Her men could talk to him. See if they could get him to tell them where he was from and why he was here. She could only hope for his own sake that his reasons were not underhanded. That he wasn't here to kill her. A mistake he would only make once when her men gained hold of him.

"Tell Niccolo that he has full authority to question the man as much as he needs to find out the truth. No physical persuasion, you understand. Not unless he's working for my uncle. Only then can Niccolo use force," she said, striding over to the chair before the fire and taking a seat, pouring herself a cup of tea.

"Yes, Miss Holly. I shall tell Niccolo right away."

Holly leaned back in her chair and slipped her feet up beside her. The sound of the rain patting the window soon turned into a deluge that made her view of the outdoors blurry. The English weather was one element she would not miss, having lived in the Mediterranean, the warmth that accompanied such living was one aspect she would be happy to return to.

She trusted her men to find out exactly who the mystery man was and where he was from.

And if at all possible, send him back from whence he came so she could get on surviving the next two months before her return to Atharia and not concern herself with anything other than that.

CHAPTER 3

*W*ith his memory restored after a good night's rest, Drew lay still, listening to the men in the alley of the stable. They spoke of a woman named Miss Holly, one of the men's instructions whispered and beyond his hearing.

He cocked his eye open a little, making out the room where he'd been placed. The woolen blankets itched, irritating his skin, and the mattress was no better than the wooden floor beneath it. For a moment, Drew regretted leaving Sotherton. Not that he regretted doing as Miss Landers asked. They would not suit, and he would be better off, allowing her the time she needed to elope and remove the threat of a marriage neither of them wanted.

The mention of Atharia, a small country that sat off the coast of Italy, caught his attention. He did not move, merely listened as the men spoke of an attack against a princess, whomever that may be. He frowned, wondering why the men would be bothered with a woman and family that was thousands of miles away.

Odd behavior indeed.

A recollection of her sat at the edge of his mind. Of a woman with long, chocolate locks and a face as sweet as a sea nymph looking over him teased his senses. Who was that woman? Had he dreamed her when he was so near to death?

Drew rubbed his jaw, sitting up. He needed to find out where he was, and with any luck, these people who had found him would help him travel to his friend's home where he was headed.

"The lad may be one of the henchmen sent by the regent king. We cannot trust him, nor can we allow him to leave until we know he has not led anyone here to hurt the princess or is the assassin himself."

One of the men scoffed. "He's a strapping lad, but nothing that we could not eliminate. I do not think he has anything to do with Atharia or the crown."

Drew frowned, unsure if he agreed with the notion that he would be easily removed as if nothing more than a trifling weed in a garden. He'd ridden horses before he could run, trained at Gentleman Jacksons, and was an expert at fencing. Not to mention his eye was accurate when it came to shooting. Granted, he'd never had a duel or shot another human being before, but he had shot game and never missed.

"Even so, Miss Holly wants him watched."

"Very good, sir," the man said, the sound of footsteps on the wooden floorboards telling Drew they had gone on with whatever duties they had. Miss Holly? Was that the woman who had rescued him? That she was mentioned in the same breath as this princess whose life was apparently in jeopardy… Did that mean they were one and the same?

The door to the stall in which he sat slid open and in ducked a large, dark-skinned man, his hair as black as the night and the large scar traveling down one side of his face from his eye to his chin was thick enough to have warranted death on a mortal.

A lucky man indeed to have survived such a blow.

"Good, you're awake. Come, Miss Holly wanted to see you when you were conscious."

The man left just as quick and, standing, Drew checked his trews, happy to find them on. He glanced about the space, spying his shirt and jacket laid over a nearby chair. He slipped them on quickly, following the behemoth of a man as he started out the stable doors.

His skin prickled, and Drew knew he was being watched. He looked over his shoulder as he stepped outside, seeing a whole army of men of similar girth and height as the man he followed. They looked like an army of berzerkers just waiting until their bloodlust put them into a furor.

Drew wasn't a small man, but he felt a little out of his league against these behemoths. The house was a large country home, nothing like Sotherton, his own, but still, a home that a country gentleman or squire may dwell within. He was sure he had seen it before but could not place the name right at this moment.

The golden stone walls and glistening windows gave the house a welcoming feel, completely opposite to the men who stood at the door, arms crossed, their eyes set upon him with unwavering annoyance.

Drew lifted his chin, passed the guards, and entered the building. Inside, the household staff went about their business, a distinctive smell of cooking meat wafted through the house, and his stomach rumbled, the reminder that he'd not eaten well for a couple of days.

The berzerker started toward a room that faced the

front of the house and gestured for Drew to enter at the door. He slid past the man, hearing the door close behind him. Drew did not know if he were alone with the woman who sat behind the desk or not, but nor did he care. The pit of his stomach clenched hard, the breath in his lungs squeezed out through his lips, and he fought not to gasp at the woman who stared, unflinchingly, back at him.

With a ramrod posture and lifted chin, authority all but oozed out of every pore on her creamy, white skin. But it was her eyes, a green so alight, so bright, that he'd never before seen anything like it.

No, that was untrue. Drew had seen a similar shade on his mother's emerald ring that his father had gifted her upon their marriage.

He nodded in welcome. "You wished to see me, Miss Holly?" he stated, using the name the other men at the estate had.

She gestured for him to sit, crossing her hands on the mahogany desk before her. Her soft-pink gown hugged her ample bosom, the pretty little ribbon tied beneath her chest all but teasing his gaze to dip and take its fill.

Drew cleared his throat, forcing his eyes to stay above her neck.

"I did. I was hoping that you could tell me who you are and what you're doing here? How it is that you came to be on the beach only two miles away, only hours from death and claiming you did not know who you were?"

Drew remembered perfectly well what he was doing on that beach. The storm had come up so quickly that he had not made landfall before it crashed from above. The boat had overturned, and somehow he'd managed to swim to the shore, but no further. So exhausted from his fight to remain alive, he had, he supposed, passed out on the sand.

He studied the woman, this Miss Holly they called her, and he could not help but believe she was the princess the guards had spoken of. No one, not even his father, the duke, had guards at the front door, standing, watching, waiting for war.

"I may, I admit, have been a little muddled after my ordeal, but I'm more than aware of who I am and how I came to be on your beach. My boat overturned and I thankfully made it to shore. I apologize if my being here is troubling for you in some way."

She stared at him and he could see she was mulling over his words. Debating if he was telling the truth or not.

"The same could be asked of you, could it not?" he continued. "Your guards mentioned a princess." He gestured to the window. "From what I can see of your ample protection here, I can only assume that Miss Holly isn't your real name. Am I correct in that estimation?"

Miss Holly or the princess or whomever she was narrowed her eyes, a flicker of steel entering her green orbs. "I see my protectors have not been guarded enough when it comes to my identity."

Drew shrugged, looking about the study. He spied the large portrait of a woman above the mantel, and he remembered, finally, which stately home he was in. "Where is Lord Bainbridge? Is he in town for the Season?"

"You know Lord Bainbridge?"

"I do. Quite well, in fact, and Lady Bainbridge. I'm Drew Meyers, Marquess of Balhannah, and future Duke Sotherton. Lord Bainbridge and my father have been friends for many years. I have not seen you, however, in town this Season. I would have remembered you, I would think."

If he expected Miss Holly to blush and simper at his

compliment, he was sadly mistaken. Her lips thinned into a displeased line, and he had the oddest sensation she was angry with him. Annoyed even at his presence here or his roundabout compliments.

She sighed, sitting up straighter, if that were even possible. "You are right, Lord Balhannah. I am HRH the Crown Princess Holly of Atharia. I came over to England to enjoy a Season with my friend Lady Mary, Lord Bainbridge's eldest daughter. Circumstances have forced me to leave town and stay here for some weeks."

Drew had not been in town long this Season, choosing to return to the country instead of facing his father at every ball and party, pointing out prospective wives he ought to court. His father and his determination to see him wed had been steadily getting worse, and so it was safer for Drew to remain away from the marriage mart in London and his father's matchmaking attempts. Not that it saved him in the end when he'd organized for Miss Landers to arrive at Sotherton to marry him there instead.

A disastrous union if ever there was to be one.

Had he known London would have had the pleasure of a princess this Season and one as beautiful as the woman who sat before him, he would never have left. He took his fill of her, her thin arms and slight shoulders. A small, golden ring sat around her little finger, an emblem of some kind upon its surface. She appeared taller than most women, a fact proven to him when she stood and went over to the fire, pulling the bell cord there. A footman entered within a moment, bowing.

"You rang, Miss Holly?" he said, flicking a curious gaze toward Drew.

"A pot of tea and some sandwiches, please. Thank you."

The young lad bowed, leaving as quietly as he arrived. Drew watched the princess move back toward the desk. Her curves were all womanly and in proportion, her breasts a lovely handful. His mouth dried at the vision she made. Holy mother of God, she was devastatingly handsome. How had he not heard she was in London?

Damn his friends for keeping her presence quiet.

"And so I shall ask again, my lord. What are you doing here at Lord Bainbridge's estate? You were close to death, do you know? And arriving on my doorstep may have ended with you meeting that fate. You're a lucky man."

Drew frowned, unsure what she meant, nor did he really think telling her he'd run away like a coward because his father wanted him to marry a woman made his washing up on her shore look any more gentleman like. If anything, it made him look like a fool in retrospect. "I apologize again for my arriving here unannounced, but from what I can remember of my accident, my boat broke up on the rocks north of the beach, and I was fortunate enough to float to shore on one of the broken planks of wood. I would never intentionally intrude at any estate that I had not been invited to, I assure you. But now that I'm here, I do have a question."

She raised her perfect brow, her eyes steely and all too intelligent. There would be no fooling the woman before him. "What is that?"

"Why leave the Season? You now know why I have arrived at your doorstep, but it is a mystery to me why you are hiding away here." She paled, leaning back in her chair, watching him as one would a snake about to strike. He did not wish to alarm her with his questions, but it was odd that she would be hiding away in the country all of a sudden after enjoying the Season with her friend.

Why do such an odd thing? It made no sense.

She sighed. "I suppose there is little harm in telling you why I am here, Lord Balhannah, but be warned, once you are aware, you will not be permitted to leave until it is safe for me to allow it. So if you really do wish to know, choose your answer correctly."

It was Drew's turn to frown. Why would he be forced to stay? Odd behavior, not that it would be so very bad to be stuck at Lord Bainbridge's country estate with a princess as beautiful as the one who was before him. "Tell me the reason. I wish to know." Wish to know? He *had* to know. Nothing else mattered at that moment, not his father or his friends. Drew only knew that he had to hear from her why she was here. The thought of her being in some kind of trouble left his blood to boil. Was some gentleman trying to persuade her into marriage, or had they made advances unbecoming or unsuitable for a princess? Drew doubted there would be many advances she would accept. Whoever married the woman before him would be much higher placed in society than even he was. A duke, not a royal duke, would never have a look in.

Damn it all to hell.

"I was here in England to enjoy a Season in your society before returning to Atharia and taking up my role there. However, my uncle has decided that he enjoys being the regent king more and does not wish for me to return. Not unless it is only my body that returns and therefore laid to rest without causing any further trouble for him."

Drew's blood ran cold. "Your uncle wants you dead? Why?" he asked, baffled. He'd heard of family disagreements, but this went beyond that twofold.

"In two months, I'm of age to take the crown for myself. At one and twenty, I shall be the Queen of Atharia.

My uncle does not wish this to occur. While in London, there was an attempt on my life. I fled to the country, and no one knows of my whereabouts, other than Lord Bainbridge. Your arrival here was suspicious, and now that you know my truth, you shall not be permitted to leave until I return to my homeland."

"May I write to my father and inform him that I am well, if not tell him where I am? He will grow concerned if I do not."

"Perhaps. I shall speak to my guards regarding your request, but if it's deemed too much of a risk, then no, you shall not."

A light knock sounded on the door, and a footman entered, bringing a tray of sandwiches and steaming tea, two delicate cups with light-blue flowers on the silver tray. "Where would you like to take your repast, Miss Holly?"

"Here, at the desk, if you will." The footman did as he was bade, setting down the tea tray and pouring two cups before bowing and leaving the room, the snick of the door as it closed loud in the quiet space.

"I am sorry that you have fallen into my troubles, Lord Balhannah, but there is little to be done for it. In eight weeks, I shall sail for Atharia, and you shall be permitted to go on with your life." She picked up a cup. "How do you have your tea, my lord? With cream? Sugar?"

"Cream, please," he said, taking the cup from her. Their fingers grazed. Heat pooled low in his gut. Her hands were delicate, but this Miss Holly, as she liked to be known, was no simpering miss. There was steel that ran through her back and blood, and she was all the more attractive to him for it.

Not that he needed to lose his head over the woman. She was not for him. Too far above his status, but blast it all to hell, he would have liked the opportunity to court her, make her laugh, and have a little entertainment before she had fled London.

"Thank you," he said, taking his tea and sitting back in his chair. "So, since we're to be stuck here at Lord Bainbridge's estate, what are we to do with ourselves?"

"What do you mean?" she asked, sipping her tea.

"I mean, what have you been doing to pass the time? Other than saving gentleman who wash up on your beaches, of course." He grinned, hoping she found amusement in his words. Not just the princess, but everyone at the estate seemed on edge. The berzerkers outside certainly appeared as if ready for a deadly battle at any moment. It was disconcerting to say the least, especially to a man like Drew. He'd always thought of himself as a gentleman who liked to play and have fun in life. Nothing too weighty to lay upon his shoulders.

The woman before him was the opposite if he were any judge of character. Her life was nothing but rules and protocol, heavy responsibilities beyond owning a grand house, and having tenant farmers. She would be the ruler of a country. Its head of state—a massive weight on such slight shoulders.

"I plan, and I wait, my lord. My time for frivolity ended when I fled London. Now I must turn toward my birthright and what that entails."

A winsome look crossed her features before she blinked, and it was gone. "Do not expect your time here to be enjoyable, my lord. I think that a gentleman like you may find your time here odious in the extreme."

"With you as my host, Miss Holly, I do think you're incorrect in your assumption. I cannot think of a place I'd rather be." Drew grinned at her, wanting to make her smile, smirk, a meager lifting of lips even would have sufficed.

He gained none of those.

Disdain was what he received. A hard woman certainly, but one he hoped would one day be his friend and look upon him as someone she could trust. That at least he could give her if he could not provide her with anything else. After all, he owed her his life.

CHAPTER 4

The following afternoon Holly stood at the library windows and watched with no small amount of amusement as Lord Balhannah was shown by one of her guards how to walk about the property and keep watch on those who may try to do her harm.

Her guards had been well trained, and although Lord Balhannah would never be left on his own, to do so would not be wise. Should they be attacked by her uncle's henchmen, his lordship may be killed, and the last thing Holly needed was someone of the British aristocracy to be murdered on her time.

The parts of the grounds his lordship was tasked to watch were out near the main entrance to the estate, a position that would not be used should her uncle find her. He was too smart to walk in through the front door. Oh no, he would try to hit at her while her back was turned.

Holly sighed, walking over to the decanter of whisky and pouring herself a healthy portion. Her father's death of the year before had been hard, but the more she thought about his demise, the more she could not help but feel that it was not of a natural state.

That her father had, in fact, been murdered by his younger, selfish, jealous sibling. That her uncle had shipped her off to England within months of laying her father to rest was of equal strangeness. Not that she had not wanted to remove herself from Atharia, a place that she loved with all her heart, but a home nonetheless that was depressing and sad after the death of its favorite king and father.

Her time here in England was supposed to be three months, yet it was now almost six. Three in London and three here at Lord Bainbridge's estate after the attempt on her life that saw her flee. Never had she been so frightened in her life than the day she had been leaving her friend's London ball, and an assailant had attacked her before everyone on the street.

It was then that she realized her uncle never designed her to return to Atharia. That he intended her dead, and possibly her sisters, while he sat on the throne, a position he'd always been envious of.

Well, she would not go down without a fight. Holly finished her drink, slamming the crystal glass on the sideboard. She needed to return to Atharia, without notice and certainly no fanfare and with an army of her own to take back what was hers.

Her younger sisters—who could be alive or dead—depended on it.

Panic threatened to assail her, and she walked over to the mantel, staring at the roaring fire burning in the grate. The first thing she needed to assail herself was men—a strong, loyal army who would fight for her rights and her life.

Atharia was a small island off the coast of Italy. Independent of the European countries. Making landfall would be dangerous, and unless they did it under cover of darkness, they would be seen from miles out. Once there, she could rally an army to her cause. The people loved her, missed her, she believed. Her people would not let her down.

Holly needed to use their love, their loyalty, and remove her uncle once and for all.

He had to die. There was nothing left but that outcome.

"Miss Holly?"

She started, turned to see Lord Balhannah standing at the library door, a concerned look on his handsome face. And he was handsome, more so than she'd thought him originally when she first came upon him on the shore.

Her men were dark, muscular gods, but Lord Balhannah was the opposite. Just as tall, although perhaps a little less athletic. He was all blond godlike deliciousness that made her heart stutter. An impossibility since she could never marry a man of his rank. As it was, her future was mapped out. Her father had hoped she could marry her Greek cousin of royal blood once she was crowned. Holly had been agreeable to this idea. She always had liked Prince Gustov. He was kind and would never try to push her from her role as queen, such as her uncle was trying to do. And yet, looking at Lord Balhannah, a future English duke, she could not help but wonder what it would be like to choose someone whom she found attractive, liked, and if luck should have it, love.

Lord Balhannah, with his long, dark eyelashes over the bluest eyes she'd ever beheld, certainly had her blood pumping faster. At almost one and twenty, she often wondered what it would be like to sleep with a man.

"How old are you, my lord?" she asked, taking in his attire that was if not fashionable, at least clean and no longer torn. She could see the remnants of a gentleman beneath his workmen's clothing. The idea of what he would look like dressed for a state dinner made her stomach flutter.

"I am five and twenty, Miss Holly." He cleared his throat, looking at someplace over her shoulder and not meeting her eyes. Curious man.

"You cannot meet my gaze, my lord. Why?"

His eyes widened and met hers, and a sense of his unease thrummed through her blood. Was he intimidated by her? It was a common issue when meeting anyone other than royal blood. They often were unsure of their status or if their presence was more out of necessity than pleasure.

"I'm unsure why I cannot." He paused, a small frown between his eyes. "I suppose my only excuse is that you make me nervous. I'm also extremely uncomfortable calling you Miss Holly when I now know you to be a princess."

"Miss Holly is used primarily to keep people at ease in my presence and for security reasons. It is an odd name, I grant you, but one that must be used. My uncle has spies everywhere, and should the smallest whisper reach him of my whereabouts, it would not end well. My brush with death in London was close enough. I do not wish to suffer that fate just yet."

"That is what I'm here to see you about. I would like to offer you my services. I have trained at Gentleman Jackson's in London and know how to fight. Granted, I am not as muscular as the men who guard you, but I do know how to draw blood with a blade. My accuracy with a gun is indisputable. I would like to help you if you allow me."

Holly narrowed her eyes, wondering at the suggestion. He was young, rich, and powerful in his own right. Why would he wish to place himself in danger to save a stranger's life? His guarding the gate was enough. He did not need to do anything further. "Why would you offer such a thing? We're not known to each other well. You owe me nothing."

He threw her a half smile, and her mouth dried. Dear lord in heaven she would need to be careful with this man. He could make her forget herself and her status and merely think about all the ways she could allow him to kiss her.

"You saved my life, do not forget, so not entirely without a debt to pay in return. But there is another reason I would like to remain by your side. A selfish one on my behalf."

She raised her brow, curious to hear his reasons. A little part of her hoped it was because he liked what he saw and was man enough to say it to her face. No one ever did. No one ever stepped out of line with her and went against her will. Only Niccolo, and that was only ever because of safety reasons, nothing else.

"Tell me the reason, my lord."

He threw her a self-deprecating smile. "I suffer from a father who wishes me to marry a woman I do not love. She, in turn, is in love with someone else. A trip abroad, away from home and London, would be most useful at this time. To be in your service, my father would have no issue with it. In fact, knowing my sire, he would be most proud of my service to keep the future Queen of Atharia safe."

Holly cleared her throat, unsure what to make of his lordship's words. As for his father, well, he seemed an interesting character. She walked over to her desk, wondering if

Lord Balhannah spoke with such openness with everyone or if it were just an affliction he was saddled with after his near-drowning.

"While I sympathize with you concerning your father's plans for your future, to be by my side, guard me against those who seek to do me harm will place you in equal danger. Maybe you require further deliberations before you choose such a fate."

"Of course," he said, a rosy hue forming on his cheeks. The blush made him appear even more endearing and sweet than he had previously. "My father has a tendency to see the positive in any situation. If I were to be part of your entourage, he would be honored."

"All of this is a moot point in any case, for if you're to travel with me, you cannot tell anyone of your where-abouts. You may notify your father that you will be going abroad, but nothing else."

His lordship came farther into the room, looking about. "May I ask how your uncle hit at you while you were in London? You mentioned there has already been an attack on your welfare."

Holly thought back to that night in London, where she enjoyed a ball at Lord Bainbridge's home. The evening had been going so well, the food and company were superb, the music played as beautifully as their own musicians played back in Atharia. But the arrival of Franco, her uncle's henchman or spy as she had always termed him, told her trouble was afoot. He had watched her the whole evening, simply stood to the side of the ballroom, and glowered at her as if she were doing something wrong. As if she were an annoyance that needed eliminating.

It was only when she was leaving, climbing up in her carriage that she'd heard the hard footsteps from behind.

The icy touch of the blade had cut her gown at her breast, where he threatened to thrust it upward and pierce her heart.

However, Franco had misjudged Niccolo, her protector, and his years of fighting to remain alive in the Atharia army had taught him well. He'd moved with lightning speed, twisting Franco's arm and snapping it before Holly had the chance to turn and see who it was who attacked her. Without much noise, Niccolo walked the wailing Franco around a nearby darkened street corner and thrust the blade meant for her into the man's neck, letting him drop as if he were nothing more than an inconsequential piece of meat.

A shocking event to witness, and a small part of Holly had been struck with fear at Niccolo's ability. He was deadly, and she could only be thankful that her father had given him the post of being her guard.

"A man in London, one who worked for my uncle, tried to stab me after a ball. He was killed, and we left town that night, fearful of further attacks. So far, we've not been found, and nothing further has occurred, but we must always be cautious. I have weeks only until I am one and twenty and able to return to Atharia and take the crown. Nothing, I can assure you, will stop me from taking what is mine and serving my uncle some well-needed punishment."

Lord Balhannah stared at her, clearly lost for words at her informing him of her troubles, of her plans. If he were to have the stomach to stay close to her side, protect her as her men did, then he would have to learn that her life was not like so many others of his acquaintance.

Through the luck of birth, she had been born into royalty, and with that came responsibilities. Not just of houses and land, of tenant farmers and staff, but of a country, its people, the security and protection and well-being of everyone who lived under her care.

Her uncle only sought to rip the country's riches away from the people and line his own greedy pockets. To take a crown that he was not ever meant to inherit. To steal her country and torment the people she loved.

The fiend would not get away with his evil plan. She would die trying to repair the damage he'd caused and earn back the trust of the people of her land.

"I would like to help in any way that I can. As a peer of the realm, maybe I could help you in gaining the assistance of the English parliament, or even the crown."

"I have assistance from them both already. King George is my fourth cousin, twice removed. Even so, they can only help so far, and unfortunately, as they have informed us, they too do not know if there are more men in England like Franco. Lying in wait to strike. You being near my person will be dangerous, my lord. Are you sure you wish to embark on such a quest? You could return home after I leave, travel to London and see out the Season, perhaps even find a woman that you do find attractive and amusing to be around, marry."

The idea of Lord Balhannah paying court to other women left a disturbing taste in her mouth. To see him pay attention to a particular woman, even a faceless one in Holly's musings, did little to calm her nerves.

"I'm not looking to marry just yet, so traveling with you and ensuring you regain what has been taken from you is something that I wish to do. It would be an honor to serve you."

Holly met his gaze and read the sincerity behind his decree. She nodded. "Thank you for your service, Lord

Balhannah. I can only pray that I return you to England and your father without incident."

He grinned. "Then it is settled."

"It certainly seems so, my lord," she said, watching as he bowed and left. Holly sat on her chair, staring at the closed door he went through. She would need all the men she could gain if she were to take out her uncle. No doubt, the traitor would use Atharia's armed forces against her. She frowned. Unless she could gain their ear, talk them out of following a madman, and support the rightful heir.

Her…

The clock on the mantel clicked the hour, a mocking bell that reminded her of time and how much longer she had to wait before she made her move. Eight weeks to be exact, and then Atharia would be hers. Under her rule and protection.

CHAPTER 5

*D*rew heard the gunshot first, followed by men bellowing to each other. He climbed up the small bank that ran the edge of the lake the estate had, narrowing his eyes toward the house to see what was happening. The sight of the princess's men running for cover and aiming weapons in return to the shots fired off from the side of the house that faced the forest told Drew all he needed to know what was afoot. Fear churned in his gut at the thought of someone harming the woman who had hidden herself away from harm. No one deserved to be hunted and killed as it seemed her uncle was wont to do. How anyone could do such a thing to another living being was beyond him.

Drew dropped low in the grass, working up toward the house and making use of the few trees that dotted the landscape where he hid. More shots were fired, a couple hitting the home and sending mortar to create a plume of dust.

He peered through the grass as best he could, not able to see or make out how many men were shooting. The sound of glass breaking followed by more gunshots held Drew still a moment before the sight of a golden, gowned woman, sprinting in the direction of the beach, caught his notice. He ran back the way he came, working his way around the grounds, keeping a clear and safe distance from the house, and started for the beach. By the time he came to the shore, he'd lost her.

Where had she gone? There weren't any boats nor horses galloping away to explain her disappearance.

Frowning, he started along the dunes, keeping his head low and listening out for any approaching men. He could hear more gunshots in the distance, and he hoped to God that the staff of Lord Bainbridge were not injured. How awful for them all.

"Your Highness," he whispered, at a loss as to where she'd gone.

"In here, Lord Balhannah," a voice came from one of the dunes. He studied the land, unable to see where she hid until a camouflaged door, covered in sand and driftwood lifted, revealing a small, square space for someone to hide. "Quickly, come in here before someone sees you, and we're both killed."

He did as she bade, jumping into the small boxed room and thankful when she closed the hatch once again. For a time, they sat in quiet, listening to the battle being waged at the estate, the bellows of her men drifting to them on the sea breeze.

"Are you hurt?" he asked, hardly able to make her out in the dark space.

"No," she replied, her voice not wobbling or hesitant in this trying time.

He reached over, taking her hand, wanting to comfort

her anyway. "When they are gone, we shall return and see what help can be given."

"There will be nothing anyone can do. My uncle never leaves anyone around who can talk later."

Drew did not like the sound of such a man. They sat in wait, only the sound of their breathing in the confined space. No more gunshots rang out, and quiet descended on the estate. Drew could just make out the princess's face in the shadows, and her unease, the concern etched on her brow told him she cared for the staff of Lord Bainbridge's home and her guards.

Would any of them be alive by the end of the day?

"The rule is that if we're found and ambushed as we have been, I'm to flee. Not return and not look back. Several miles from here is an old shepherd's hut. No one lives there now, and it is mostly a ruined dwelling, but it is safe and where we shall go. If Niccolo is alive, he will meet me there within a day or two. If he does not, I know that I have lost him."

The dread in her tone gave him pause. Did this princess have feelings for her guard that went beyond his role of protector? A part of Drew did not like to consider such a thing. Not that she could have feelings for him either, he reminded himself. He may be a marquess and future duke, but that was nothing when it came to royalty.

"I will go with you and keep you safe, you have my word, Your Highness."

She sighed, bowing her head. "All those innocent people have probably lost their lives because I did not strike before my twenty-first birthday. I led those thugs directly to them all, and now there is little doubt they are all dead."

Crunching footsteps sounded on the sand outside their

den. Drew hauled Holly against him, stemming her words with a hand over her mouth. She didn't fight him, stilled and quietened in his hold, and a part of him mourned that she had learned to live with such threats and fears.

No person deserved fear to hover about their everyday life. What an awful way to live.

"Shush," he whispered against her ear, the scent of citrus wafting from her coffee-colored locks. He slipped his arm around her, holding her close, and didn't miss the shiver that ran through her body.

A man's voice, closer than Drew would like, yelled for others to keep searching, stating that the princess could not have gone too far. To check the sand dunes.

"Are there any weapons in here?" Surely, they placed something in this pit should the worst befall the estate.

"Yes, there is a box behind us that holds two flintlocks."

Drew edged backward, using his hands to find the box. He made short work getting them out, the flint and powder, priming the guns both ready for use. If they were found, at least they would kill a couple bastards before being killed themselves.

He handed one of the guns to the princess. She took it from him without a word, holding it toward the opening. They waited well into the night, where they could no longer see their own hands. The chill seeped into the space, and Drew went back to the box that held the guns, pleased to find a blanket. Still, the men searched the land. Every so often, they would hear them calling, their footsteps as they ran along the beach.

Drew wrapped a blanket about them both, pulling the princess into his arms and using his body heat to warm hers. "I know this is not appropriate, but I'm making an exception under the circumstances."

He felt her chuckle more than heard it. "I do not mind, my lord, so long as you do not care that I rest against you to sleep. I feel so very weary after today."

Drew rubbed her back, offering comfort in any way he could. He couldn't imagine the pain she felt at losing the only people who had kept her safe—the staff at the estate who seemed quite taken by her and honored to care for her also.

"May I ask something else of you?"

She adjusted in his hold, snuggling up to his side, and Drew had to admit to enjoying having her in his arms. Her body was feminine and well-proportioned. The type of lady who turned gentlemen's heads, his included. How he wished to have seen her in London. What a beautiful sight she must have been to be behold.

"Of course," she replied, pulling the blanket about her shoulders.

"My name is Drew, as you are already aware. May I call you by your given name? Your Highness and Miss Holly do not seem appropriate in this situation."

"It does not, does it?" she mumbled against his chest where her head lay. He liked the warmth of her breath on him. It had been too long since he'd enjoyed the comforts of sleeping with a woman. Not that he would ever try to court the woman in his arms, but something about her made him unable to walk away, to leave her to her own devices and life. He would see her safely returned to Atharia. If he did nothing else in his life, he would do this.

"You may call me Holly."

Holly. A sweet name for a woman with so much strength. He was in awe of her. He leaned against the side of the pit, shutting his eyes, the gun safely beside him and Holly on his other side, safe in his arms. They would get out of this situation, travel to the shepherd's hut, and regroup from there. He could always take her to his home. No one even knew of his being at Lord Bainbridge's estate. They would not be able to track her to his Sotherton.

Drew thought about the particulars, what he could tell his father of the strange woman who slept beneath the ducal roof. He could not tell him the truth, but he had to think of something that would suffice.

Weariness swamped him, and he closed his eyes. If they made it through the night without detection, then he would give the idea more thought. Only then would he mention it to Holly, the woman in his arms, a princess. Drew doubted he would ever wrap his head around that truth.

CHAPTER 6

*H*olly awoke to the sound of silence the following morning, eerily still, not even a breath of wind dared blow in from the sea. She blinked, remained still, and reveled for the small amount of time that she'd slept in Drew's arms. He was warm, asleep, and half-lying over her. Sometime through the night, they must have moved and used each other to make themselves more comfortable.

His heart beat a steady rhythm beneath her ear. She closed her eyes, wishing life could be smooth, as reliable as the sound of his heart. They would have to move today, seek shelter elsewhere. The shepherd's hut would do for now, but what then? Without her guards' support, it would be almost impossible to survive returning to Atharia to take the throne.

All her plans were now ripped to shreds.

Drew moved beneath her, attempting to sit up and letting out a disgruntled groan as he did so. "Remind me not to lie in that position again. Oh my, I'm so sore."

Holly pushed herself up, stretching and smoothing her

tangled hair. A small piercing of light drifted through from the wooden hatch above them, and she moved to see if she could see anyone outside, quiet and in wait for her to appear.

"We'll leave today. Let me see if there are any survivors and make sure your uncle's men have left. No matter what you hear, do not leave this den."

Holly wasn't stupid enough to argue the point. It was imperative she stay alive. Not just because she did not want to die, but because her people's happiness depended on her returning home and removing them from her uncle's dictatorship rule.

She watched as Drew went to the door, listening and pushing it open, just the smallest crack. Sunlight bathed the small space, allowing her to take stock of where they had slept. It was littered with cobwebs, the fact that she was glad to have not noticed before. Other than the small box holding the weapons and a blanket, there was little else here.

Drew reached back, pocketing one of the flintlocks, and then lifted the door. Holly squinted, hoping beyond anything that no shot rang out, that no shout of men sounded as he stepped free of the space.

With one last look back at her, he dropped the lid, and once more, she was alone. For how long she could not say. The time felt like hours, but it could have been only minutes all told. No sounds of shouting men or gunfire met her ears, and it gave her hope that her uncle's men had fled. She would worry about where they went from here later. All she could hope for right now was that her guards were unharmed and the staff of Lord Bainbridge had survived, although the possibility of that was scarce.

She gasped, startled when the lid to the den was lifted,

and Drew stood before her, his face ashen, his eyes a little startled. A horse threw its head about behind him. She stood, reaching for his hand when he leaned down toward her to help her out.

"What was it like back at the house? Please tell me there were survivors."

Drew was silent a moment, checking that the saddle strap was tight before hoisting himself up. "One footman is dead in the foyer, the rest of the staff had locked themselves in the cellar. Your uncle's men did not search there, it would seem. I cannot tell you how sorry I am that this has happened to you and the estate."

The world spun, and she clasped the bridle of the horse, stopping herself from falling over. An innocent footman was dead? One life was too many. The thought made her stomach roll, and she turned, heaving up her accounts onto the sand dunes. She had done this, brought on this tragedy to Lord Bainbridge's people. However would she gain forgiveness for bringing such pain to the family and the footman's loved ones? A cross that she would bear forever.

"My guards? Did you see any of them?"

Drew reached out a hand for her, and reluctantly Holly took it, knowing she had to leave. If she were ever to make her uncle pay for this crime, she could not die here and now. Drew hoisted her up behind him on the horse. He kicked the mount, and they raced down onto the beach to gallop along the shore where the sand was harder.

"Two of the guards were dead, the others I could not find. I do not know where they may have been. I did check the house fully, to ensure no one was tied up anywhere. I shall have to leave word for Lord Bainbridge of what has happened so he can return home."

Holly's vision blurred, and she leaned into Drew's back. Where was Niccolo? Had he survived? He was her most trusted and strong guard. She could not move forward without his help.

She did not reply to Drew's words, no retorts could better what had happened. How had they found out where she was living? And why did they feel the need to kill innocent staff? Bastards!

They rode for a good two hours before Drew slowed the horse. Holly glanced over his shoulder and spied the shepherd's cottage, dilapidated, half its timber slat roof missing. They would not be able to light a fire here either, just in case her uncle's men were in the area and knew of the normally vacant dwelling.

"We're almost there. I see a small lean-to for the horse, which is fortunate, he too shall rest well over the night. As for us," Drew said, little mirth in his tone, "I think tonight shall be decidedly worse than last evening."

Holly could not agree more. The closer they came to the building, the more she wanted to run in the opposite direction. It was worse than she'd first thought, no glass in any of the windows, and there was a distinct odor of sheep or cattle as if the animals used the house for their own purposes.

Delightful...

Drew pulled the horse up before the front door, and for a moment, they both stared at the building. Never in her life had she ever fallen so low. Never had anything ever struck at her so severely as her uncle had yesterday and now this today.

She closed her eyes a moment, rallying her strength. She would not let him get the better of her. She was stronger than that. Her father made her determined and she'd be damned if she'd let her sniveling, conniving uncle get the better of her or her people. She would go forward, one step at a time, and fight him with everything she had left.

Drew reached behind, helping her slide off the horse, and she stood still a moment, allowing her legs to adjust to being off the horse. Her body ached, stiff and tired, both physically and mentally, and all she craved was a long, soaking bath. Her stomach rumbled, reminding her she had not eaten since lunchtime yesterday. There was little doubt in her mind that the shepherd's cottage held no food or water.

Drew jumped down off the horse, walking it into the small shelter before tying it to a post. "There is some old hay here, thankfully. The horse shall eat at least." He paused at the shelter's opening, looking about the land. "I'm going to walk about, see if I can find some water. There must be a stream or river nearby. No one would build a hut here otherwise."

Holly watched as Drew collected an old, discarded bucket from the front of the house before he walked off in search of water. She started toward the building, hoping that perhaps the inside wasn't as bad as she expected.

The ground was uneven, and the silk slippers she had been wearing the day before when her uncle's men had attacked her home were no barrier to the rocks and prickers that littered the unkept ground. The house and land did not look to have been used for many years. Cobwebs and animal droppings littered the rotten wooden deck. Inside was not much better.

It was atrocious.

Holly stood at the door and stared at the room where they were to sleep this evening. Perhaps they would be better off continuing on, but then, the horse would struggle, and with two riders these past miles, it needed a well-earned break.

The house was a single room, a small cupboard sat against what she supposed was a window, a wash trough still sitting on its bench. A kitchen, perhaps? A cot lay at the other end of the room, ripped, decaying curtains hung from an equally rotten pole. Tonight would be cold, and Holly wished she'd had the sense to bring the small blanket they'd huddled under last night.

A sound outside made her jump, and she turned to see Drew striding toward her, a bucket hanging at his side and sloshing water over his boots. She stared at him a moment, hoping she could trust him with her secret. Hoping that it wasn't him who had brought her uncle to her doors.

She cringed at the thought. Surely not. He had washed up half-dead on the beach, he knew Lord Bainbridge for heaven's sake. Lord Balhannah had done nothing to make her think he sided with her uncle. Had he wished her harm, he would have opened the small den they huddled in yesterday and told her uncle's men where they were hiding.

He had not.

At that moment, Drew glanced up, throwing her a half smile, and she got a sense of what he would be like in a ballroom, miles from here, and the troubles surrounding her. What the women of the famous London *ton* would think of him and his handsome face, cutting cheekbones, and straight nose. A perfectly proportioned gentleman that, even in his disheveled state, could make a woman's heart beat fast.

A princess's thoughts were no different.

CHAPTER 7

She stepped into the room, giving Drew leave to enter. He glanced about quickly, spying the cupboard near the window and placing the water there. "I think we'll have to risk a fire this evening. There is weather coming in from the west, will turn chill tonight. We have the flintlocks, and I'll gather some dirt to place over the fire should we suspect anyone is about."

Holly nodded, going over to the bucket. "Do you think the water is safe to drink?" Come to mention it, she really needed to excuse and relieve herself before she drank anything more.

"The bucket wasn't in too bad condition, and I cleaned it thoroughly before filling it with water. I saw another where the horse is stabled, I shall collect it soon and give the horse some water as well." He rolled his shoulders, glancing about the space, and she didn't miss the grimace over what he saw. "Did you want to walk down to the river with me to wash up a little?"

"I cannot, my shoes are not suitable for hiking about

the land. I will be well enough until we find suitable accommodation elsewhere."

"Talking of such," he said, pulling out two chairs that were tipped over on the dirt floor, not bothering to remove the dust from its wood before he sat. "I have been thinking about what we should do. Your next step, and I think I have found a solution." He gestured to the chair for her to sit also.

With her gown already ruined and well past stained, Holly sat, promising once again that her uncle would pay for her current conditions. "What do you suggest?" she asked.

"You should return to Sotherton with me, to my family estate, regroup from there, hire new men if need be, and travel to Atharia when the time comes. My estate has a deep harbor, we can have ships port there. Not to mention no one knows of my being at Lord Bainbridge's estate and nor will they if you write to him about what happened there. I can have the letter posted from London to throw off any spies who may be watching the mail to his lordship."

Holly bit her lip, thinking over his idea. It certainly appeared sound enough, and at this time, she really had no other option but to do as he suggested. Her men were lost to her at present. Who knows how many survived or had been captured? Niccolo was missing, and even though she hoped that he would meet her here as they had planned should something terrible befall them, something told her he would not. If he had died, all that she could pray for was that it was fast, and he had not suffered.

Her guards were like family to her, older brothers whom she knew as well as her own sisters. To think of them slaughtered in cold blood, for no reason other than an old man's greed, left a hollow void in her chest.

"Very well, I shall come with you to Sotherton, but what will you tell your father? Will he not be scandalized that you've brought a woman home with you?"

Drew swallowed, a pensive look on his face. "He will be surprised, but that is the next thing that I wished to speak to you about. Are you open to the idea of us being married? Not in truth," he quickly added when she blanched, "but just for the time that you're living at Sotherton? My father will be nothing but pleased should I return home with a wife, and we can make up some title and family history for you. Maybe an Italian heiress recently returned to enjoy the London Season."

Holly mused over the idea. It could work, but what would be the terms of this falsified marriage? "Will we have separate rooms, my lord, or am I expected to share your bed for the sake of your father's morals?"

A light blush stole across Drew's cheeks, and she bit back a grin. "You shall have a separate suite of rooms, Your Highness. I would not expect anything from you, of course. We may, however, need to hold hands at some point in time, or at least appear besotted with each other."

Holly chuckled. It would be no hardship feigning a likeness for this man. What a diversion he had become in the two short days she had known him. All she could hope was that he not only diverted her from her problems, but helped her solve them as well. Enabled her to return home and take the crown that is rightfully hers.

"You know that I cannot stay forever. At some point, you will need to tell your father that we must leave for Atharia. Of course, I shall not return with you. How will you explain it to your sire then?"

"I will tell him the truth at that point. You will have the crown and your country back by then, and there will be no more reason for secrecy."

"I only have weeks left before the crown becomes legally mine to take. I cannot delay returning to Atharia, my lord, not just because of my uncle's dividing and cruel rule but also because my two sisters are under his care. I fear for their safety. I am unmarried and without a child. Should I die, he would have no qualms killing the two people next in line."

"Why do you think he has not done so already?" Drew asked.

Holly hoped he had not. The thought of Alessa and Elena cold in the ground sent a chill down her spine, her heart to stop. "I do not know that he has not hurt them. I have little doubt they are under lock and key, but I think he would be a fool to hurt them. He needs them at the moment to show the people that although the country is under his rule, his brother's children are safe. I'm in England, miles from my people's eyes, he does not care what happens to me here. Should I fall on his sword, he can merely announce that I have died of some disease or tragic accident while abroad."

The concern on Drew's face reminded her that her situation was precarious and not without danger. She was a strong woman, an intelligent willful one, but going up against her uncle and his army would not be an easy feat. Some days, days like today, where she had to huddle in a shepherd's hut, made her question whether she'd be able to accomplish her goal.

She should never have left Atharia, as her uncle suggested. Had she known he would do as he had, she would never have left her homeland and allowed the country to fall into his corrupt hands.

"I will go down and fetch more water and look for some firewood and then return. If you're comfortable, see what you can make of the bedding situation before we lose sunlight."

"I can do that, my lord. If you see anyone, do not try to confront them. My uncle's men, my men, are ruthless killers when the need arises. No amount of Gentleman Jackson boxing lessons will save you against them."

"I have my gun, but I promise I shall not be long or do anything foolish."

Holly watched Drew leave, going over to the bucket and taking a sip using her hands. An action that she'd never had to do before in her life. It was degrading for a princess.

Going to the door, she watched as Drew disappeared over the ridge of the hill. Needing to relieve herself, she stepped outside, going around the opposite side of the hut. Holly hoisted up her skirts as best she could and, squatted. She looked about, hoping against hope that no one came into view and saw her. That the future queen of Atharia was crouching in the soil outside a dilapidated cottage like some animal, made her eyes smart with tears.

She bit her lip hard, stemming her upset. She would not cry. She was stronger than that, and she needed to remain so to win this battle against her uncle. A footman had died on her watch, an innocent servant. Others, no doubt, were traumatized by the event. Their lives would not be in vain just because she did not have the backbone to fight her uncle.

Finishing her business, she stood and walked back inside, staring at the bed that looked like it hadn't been used for fifty years. The bedding was ripped and dirty. Animals had slept on it, and droppings littered the rotten mattress. They would not be able to use it, but perhaps it could be set up against the window at one end of the cottage to stop any light escaping from the building.

She collected the linens, ripping them up into smaller pieces, and placing them where the fire would be laid in the room's center. If they could not find any small wood for kindling, at least this linen could be used.

Holly busied herself as much as she could while waiting for Drew. She picked up rubbish to burn, hung an old blanket stained with something she did not wish to contemplate over the window that the kitchen sat before. Hopefully, this would help in stopping the drafts. As it was, again tonight, they would have to sleep close together. It would be the only way in which to stay warm.

The idea of lying against Drew's chest was not an unwelcome thought. He was strong, tall, handsome as sin, and kind. She just hoped beyond hope that he had not led her uncle to her. Holly dismissed the unhelpful thought. He could not do such a thing. Her mind was running away with her again, making her see ghosts and threats where there were none.

Footsteps sounded outside, and she glanced up just as Drew stepped back into the hut, a load of wood in his arms. "This will hopefully see us through the night, but I would not recommend we stay here a second. With no food and little shelter, we would be best to push on to Sotherton."

"If Niccolo was to join me here, I should think he would've done so already. That he is not here, I do not think he survived." The thought of her most trusted guard lying dead somewhere on Lord Bainbridge's property made her want to cast up her accounts. He did not deserve such a death. He was supposed to live, to help her make her uncle pay.

"Have you thought about the guise of playing my wife?"

"I have," she said, leaning down to help him build up the fire, placing some of the ripped bedding around the wood. "I think it is a sound idea. We shall tell your father that we married in secret several months ago. You've not been away from home long enough to have traveled to Gretna and back to have a new wife, or procured a special license. If we have separate rooms and you do not try anything beyond what you stated, I am in agreement."

He chuckled, meeting her gaze across the unlit fire. "I promise not to attempt to kiss you, Your Highness, no matter how tempting. Your reputation is safe with me."

Holly cleared her throat at the mention of kissing. "Yes, well, let us hope it is. Secondly," she continued, "with no one knowing you were at the estate, I think it shall be safe to use Holly as my given name, but we need to create a surname. Perhaps I could be an heiress you met in London last Season. Our backstory must be solid to halt your father from thinking we're lying."

"Maybe a distant cousin to Lady Mary, Lord Bainbridge's daughter? You were staying at her estate, after all. It would make sense to stay as similar to your circumstances as possible."

"That is true," she mused, staring down at the makings of their fire and not missing the fact that the air had turned sharp or that the light had dimmed in the cottage. "I will not be circulating in society at your father's estate in any case. We shall use the name Devereux as I did previously. However, we will need to come up with a ruse as to why your father cannot tell anyone of our whereabouts. Perhaps we can say we wish for privacy for several weeks, to enjoy our marriage alone without the gossiping *ton* talking about us."

"We can do that, of course," he said. Drew stood and went about the room, looking around the fireplace that had unfortunately caved in and was unusable. He searched in a couple of old tins atop the mantel. "Ah-ha, there is still some tinder and flint here. Now we shall have a fire."

Coming back to kneel beside her, he flicked the steel striker against the flint, and the tinder caught, along with the wood Holly had wrapped with old bedding.

Heat met her skin, a little comfort in their miserable surroundings. The night would be long, but at least they would be warm.

"Before I close the door, do you wish to use the retiring room, Your Highness?"

Holly chuckled, shaking her head at his attempt to lighten the mood. "You mean the ground outside? No, thank you. I'll be fine for the night."

Drew closed the door. Thankfully with the roof missing some of its wooden slats, the smoke drifted up and out of their eyes. "Thank you for looking after me, my lord. I know I am asking a great deal of you."

"You saved my life. I am merely doing what is right and what anyone would do in the same situation. You do not need to thank me." He sat fully on the ground, leaning up against one of the wooden walls. The dust settled on his coat. His shirt, too, was stained from the day's activities. Holly looked down at her gown that bore the mark of a day on horseback and the previous night in a hole.

Her mind wandered to the servants of Lord Bainbridge's home, and her heart ached for their suffering.

How would she ever face his lordship again after bringing such horror to his doors?

"Tell me about your home. Your sisters," Drew said.

Holly met his gaze over the firelight. They were as warm as the heat from the flames, kind and giving. Here, in this hobble of a house, far away from the opulent life she was used to, she did not feel unsafe. In fact, with Drew, she felt more relaxed than ever before, even with her uncle's men pursuing her at every turn.

Something about the man told her he would fight to save her life. That when he declared he would look after her, he meant it.

"They are younger, as beautiful inside as they are out. There is only a year between each of us, so we are very close. They mean everything to me, and I long to see their faces again. I would have already been home had my life not been threatened in London."

"Are they married or betrothed?"

"No, our marriages must be one of state. Of royal blood. It is what has always been done, but I know my sisters do not like this family tradition." She smiled, remembering all the arguments they had over the right to choose their own husbands. "They wish for marriages of love. When I am queen, I shall give them that choice, even if it is not a possibility for myself."

"Why not you? As queen, surely no one would naysay you?"

She shrugged, playing with a little twig that sat before her crossed legs. "There are anticipated expectations on my shoulders. I cannot disappoint my people, not after leaving them for the past few months under the care of my uncle, who has failed miserably."

Drew stared at her for a moment. Holly could see he

was mulling over her words. A look of disappointment crossed his features, and she wondered at it. Why would a marquess from England be concerned with her future marital status? Was the lord a romantic at heart? Or, perhaps, he was judgemental over her decree to marry a man of royal blood. He wasn't so far beneath her in status, he was a lord and future duke after all, even so, a man of his caliber wasn't good enough for a crown princess. Unfortunate as that was.

Tiredness swamped her, and she yawned, covering her mouth with her hand. "Would you mind if I slept next to you again, my lord? I'm feeling very fatigued and would like to sleep."

"Of course." He stood, coming over to her and sitting beside her on the dirty, dusty floor. Without asking, he pulled her into his side, leaning back against the wall of the hut. His hand idly rubbed along her arm, sending goose-bumps to rise on her skin. For a time, Holly stared at the flames licking the wood in the fire. She would never forget her time here with his lordship. Maybe even in her dotage, she'd tell her grandchildren of the time she had to flee for her life and was rescued by a peer of England's realm.

Her eyes grew heavy, her ability to think at all waning. "Will we reach your father's estate by tomorrow evening, do you think?"

"I think so." Holly placed her head on his chest, his voice, deep and gravelly with his own exhaustion, rumbled against her ear. She had to admit that his voice was really quite disturbing in all the improper ways. Reminded her of a few times back in London when the gentlemen thought to try their wiles on her. Not that Drew was doing any such thing, but in his case, his muffled voice relaxed and soothed her soul. Made her forget her troubles and simply revel in the sound.

"Dream of a long, hot bath and clean sheets, Your Highness. I will push our mount tomorrow to ensure we arrive at Sotherton. I will not allow you to sleep so rough again."

"It is not so very bad," she lied, adjusting herself when a pebble dared to poke her though her gown and injure her hip. "But I will be glad to be at least safer than we are now." Holly looked up at Drew, meeting his hooded gaze. "I do not wish to bring trouble to your family doors either, my lord. I do not think that my heart could stand another such event."

"It will not. No one will know you're there. Now sleep," he ordered, his fingers pushing a lock of hair from her brow. The scene was intimate, more so than she'd ever experienced in her life, and she quickly lay back onto his chest, needing to cease gazing into his stormy blue eyes. There was no future here, not in England and not in this man's arms. However, there was room for them to be friends, which she was certain they were fast becoming.

Anything more than that was impossible. She was the future queen of Atharia. That was her first and only love and her only goal.

CHAPTER 8

As promised, Drew pushed their mount hard the following day north, only stopping to rest twice and water the horse and to allow Holly to relieve herself. Unfortunately, while taking care of business beside a large oak, Holly had smelled the unfortunate odor that had started to permeate from her skin.

The knowledge both horrified and humbled her. When she returned home to Atharia and had the power in her hands, she would do more for the poor. For those who lived in squaller and struggled with everyday necessities. Living off the land, not having the basic needs for life, water, food, hygiene, and adequate clothing for the climate was not a struggle she would allow her people to face alone.

Drew pulled the horse to a stop atop a hill that over-looked both the vast ocean and his home, Sotherton. The sight made the breath in her lungs catch. It was simply beautiful and perfectly placed. Never before had she seen a house so happily situated. Even her own palace that over-looked the Mediterranean sea was a little off the coast. This house appeared to be perched nearer to the water's edge, an extensive garden and parkland making it a private oasis.

"It's beautiful," she said, unable to tear her eyes from the sight of it. Sandstone walls and a gray-tiled roof glittered in the afternoon sun. The land was green and lush, the ocean calm and a perfect blue that would tease the sky itself.

Drew glanced over his shoulder, pride filling his eyes. "I do love it here, and I want you to feel safe and welcome. Father will understand once he hears we're married. You will not be harmed while at Sotherton."

"Thank you," she said, squeezing him a little about the waist.

He kicked the mount, and they started down the hill, a leisurely pace now, allowing the horse to gain its breath and rest a little. "I will show you about when we've rested a couple of days. I know you must be exhausted."

"Thank you, that is very kind. I will also need some letters sent as soon as possible to Lord Bainbridge and my contact in London, letting them know of the events that have taken place. My contact will join me here and regroup."

"Can he be trusted?" Drew asked her.

"Of course," Holly said without question. Marco was Niccolo's brother, and he would search for her missing guards and ensure she was well prepared for her journey back to Atharia in a matter of weeks. All she could pray was that Niccolo would be found and returned to her. He wanted her uncle removed from the throne as much as she did. After being under his command before being sent with her to England, Niccolo understood her uncle's cruelty better than most.

They rode down to the estate, and Drew pointed out a

few features that piqued Holly's interest. The beach was a place she found soothing and good for the soul to think things through and relax. She looked forward to visiting Drew's.

She observed ancient oaks that were planted by his several-times-removed grandfather, The estate, which had been built beside an old Roman fort and still had remnants standing today. The manicured, fragrant, and simply stunning gardens that his mother had planted during her time here.

Sotherton was, in Holly's opinion, breathtakingly wonderful.

"Is your mother at home?" she asked, hoping another woman may be present, a welcome reprieve when always surrounded by men.

"Unfortunately, my mother passed several years ago. She was ill for quite some time before she succumbed. I think you would have liked her. She was bold and strong and capable, just as you are."

Holly smiled at the compliment, although at this very time, with her legs and back aching, her body reeking of sweat and two days of dirt, she didn't feel very strong and capable at all. She felt weak and tired, fatigued both mentally and physically, and she stank.

"I feel as though I could sleep for days," she admitted, resting her head against Drew's back. A little time later, he pulled the horse up before the house. A young stable lad ran out, taking the horse and wishing Lord Balhannah a good afternoon.

Drew reached behind and helped her alight, jumping down himself and handing the reins off to the servant. "Come, I shall introduce you to my father. Do not be nervous, he will welcome you, I'm sure."

The front doors opened, and the duke stood on the threshold. Holly smiled and soon learned that it was pointless to try to win the older man's praise. With hands-on-hips and a fierce scowl on his aged forehead, he pinned his son to the spot. "Where have you been, boy? You had better not tell me any lies, for I have had your fiancée's father here, berating me over your disappearance upon their arrival."

Drew was betrothed? Holly remembered to shut her mouth before she turned to pin Drew with one of her own glowers. "You're engaged?"

*D*rew fought not to roll his eyes. His father was beyond vexing to say such a thing, and in front of a stranger. A guest no less. "I am not engaged, and father, I left you a note as to where I was traveling. You knew very well where I was."

The duke mumbled something under his breath, and Drew pulled Holly forward. Her hand felt small and delicate in his. She did not shy away from his touch. Indeed, she held on to him with a firm grasp, even though she too was not sure of his romantic position.

"Come inside, we shall speak further. There is someone that I wish for you to meet."

For the first time, the duke's attention moved to Holly, and a contemplative light entered his eyes. He turned about, striding back into the house. Drew followed his father into his study, closing the door to ensure privacy.

"Father," he said, helping Holly to sit in a chair across from his sire's desk. "This is Holly Devereux, my wife. I'm married, congratulate me."

His father's mouth opened and closed several times, his

eyes wide in shock before he sputtered his reply. "You're what? Whatever shall I say to my old school friend, Mr. Landers?"

"I do not think Mr. Landers will be bothering you going forward. I know for certain that his daughter loved another and would be right at this very moment eloping with him. It was one of the reasons I left. I had already married, you see, and I knew from a letter I received from Miss Landers that she did not wish to marry me, so I could not stay. I hope you're not angry."

"My being angry or not will depend on who you married, boy and when. You cannot in the few days that you've been missing have traveled to Gretna and back."

Drew chuckled, seating himself beside Holly and taking her hand. "I married Holly some weeks ago before I returned from London. It was a private and small ceremony utilizing a special license. We did not tell anyone of our nuptials since we did not wish for gossip. I hope you understand."

His father leaned back in his chair, steepling his fingers. His attention snapped to Holly, and the hard edges and angles of his face softened a little. A good sign in Drew's estimation. "What is your name, and who is your family, my dear? I hope my son has been treating you well. From the looks of both your attire, you're far from presentable."

"I'm Holly Devereux, as Drew mentioned, and a distant cousin to Lady Mary, Lord Bainbridge's eldest daughter. We had a little trouble with my carriage, you see, on our travels here. We were set upon by bandits, and they stole everything except my horse. I suppose they thought that we could at least keep him if nothing else."

"Oh, you poor dears." His father stood, going over to the decanter of brandy and pouring them both a glass. He came back to them quickly, handing them their drinks. "You must be traumatized by what you've suffered."

Drew stood, patting his father on the shoulder, calming him. "We're fine, father, merely tired and unpardonably dirty. A good night's rest and some food will set us back to rights, I'm sure."

"I shall have a bath sent up to your room. You shall have my suite, my boy. Now that you're married and have a wife, I do not need the ducal apartments." His father bustled over to the fireplace and rang for a servant.

Their butler, Thomas, entered, bowing. "Your Grace?"

"Ah, Thomas, have the maids clean out the ducal apartments and move my son into the room post-haste. He's married and should therefore have that suite of rooms. I shall move into the east wing. It has better light in any case and the duchess's favorite part of the house. I shall be most pleased there."

"Very good, Your Grace. We shall do so immediately."

"You do not have to move out of your room," Holly said, throwing Drew a beseeching look. "Tell him, Drew, that he does not need to decamp on our behalf."

"Of course, I do, my dear. You're going to be the future Duchess of Sotherton, and as such, the rooms are yours. You may decorate them as you see fit when you're recovered from your trying few days."

Drew smiled at Holly. He himself feeling the pinch of guilt for allowing his father to believe they were married and happy. That Holly was going to stay at Sotherton for the rest of her life. His father would be devastated to find out it was all a ruse, but there was little for it. She had saved his life, and he would save hers in return. A gentleman never allowed a woman to succumb to a bully, a murderer like her uncle.

When his father knew of her truth, of who she really was, he would forgive him. And perhaps, one day in the distant future, they could travel to Atharia and visit Holly and her family. The start of a lifelong friendship.

"That is very generous of you, Father," Drew said, sitting beside Holly again. "There is also something else we would ask of you."

His father rejoined them, the pleasure on his features over his son's supposed marriage made Drew feel worse than he already did about lying to him. No matter that it was for the best, the news that they were not would hurt him. "Of course, anything, son. With such good news that I have received today, I would deny you nothing."

Oh, dear Lord, it could not be any worse.

"We need the knowledge that Holly and I are here at Sotherton to remain unknown by our family and friends. As I explained, I married Holly several weeks ago, and we have not had much time alone since then. I do not wish for the *ton* and the gossiping matrons of the *ton* to hear of our news and speak of nothing else. They can have this tidbit of gossip next Season, not this one."

His father frowned, taking in them both. "If that is what you wish, I shall not write to your mother's sister in town. But by doing so, I shall leave it up to you to tell her you married without her knowledge or attendance. That is one battle I do not wish to face."

Drew chuckled. "I shall tell Aunt Rosemary, of course." He reached over to Holly and took her hand, startled to find it chilled. "I think some hot soaking baths are in order, Father. We're quite tired."

"Of course, how selfish of me to keep you both so long when you require rest. Settle yourselves before the fire, and

I shall have the baths drawn for you both. You may use guest suites while the ducal room is cleaned and cleared."

"Thank you, Father."

The duke left them then, heading into the foyer and yelling out for Thomas. Drew helped Holly over to the fire, the heat a welcome reprieve from the previous evening when it had been quite chill, even in the warmer months.

"So, I am to sleep in the same bed as you, Drew? That is not what we agreed," Holly said, her mouth in a displeased line.

Drew did not like that she was mad at him, but what else was left for to him to say? A married couple who did not share the same room would look odd. "Of course not. There is a daybed in the ducal suite. I shall sleep there. There will be talk if we do not, and that is the last thing that you need."

"Very well, I shall acquiesce in this case, but you should know that I'm not in any way in approval of this."

"I know you are not. I promise you are safe with me, Your Highness." Reputation and life combined.

CHAPTER 9

With one last glance at Drew, she turned to face the fire, watching as the flames licked the wood to charred ash. How she longed for a bath, to wash the grime and remnants of travel off her skin. To soothe her aching bones and rest knowing that for the moment, she was safe. Tomorrow she would write to Marco in London and have him come to her. With no sign of Niccolo, that was the only option open to her.

The door opened, and a maid bobbed a quick curtsy. "My lord and lady, your baths are ready. If you would follow me, please."

Drew stood, holding out his arm for her to take. Without thought, she took it. She truly wondered if she would make it up the stairs, so weary were her legs.

"A bath will soon set you to rights, and you'll be able to plan and move forward with your life," he whispered, his words grazing her ear and eliciting a shiver across her skin. His very nearness did odd things to her, things that she'd never experienced before.

Not that she had much experience with men. Certainly,

no one was able to court her being the crown princess to the Atharia throne. Her marriage would be, in a sense, picked by what was best for the country, not so much her heart.

If she were to choose a husband for herself, she could imagine picking someone like Drew. He was kind and caring, two traits most important to her, and also as an added premium, extremely handsome. She cast her eyes over his profile. His face was what made hearts and fans flutter in society, no doubt. Holly smiled a little, unable to hide the fact she was happy she must feign being married to the gentleman. She would enjoy her few weeks being his wife, in name only. To taste a life that was otherwise closed to her. A normal life, as a countryman's spouse.

"I will start first thing in the morning with my letters." They came to the first-floor landing and followed the maid along a wide, long corridor. Multiple doors opened on either side of the passage, private rooms or parlors, Holly did not know. They came partway up the aisle, and the maid turned, gesturing to a room. "We've assigned Jane to you, my lady. She will be your lady's maid and can help you bathe if you please."

"Thank you." Reluctantly, Holly let go of Drew's arm, heading into the room with green silk wallpaper and dark mahogany furniture. It was an impressive guest suite and made her wonder what the ducal rooms looked like.

The door closed behind her, but she did not care. All that her mind could focus on was the steaming, deep bath that had been brought up and set before the fire.

The maid dipped into a curtsy, smiling. "I'm Jane, my lady. Would you like me to help you with your gown?"

"Yes, thank you," she said, coming closer to the bath and the heat of the fire. Holly turned, and Jane made short work of the hooks and eyes at the back of her gown, letting her patterned muslin dress to fall to the floor. Her petticoat and stays were next, followed by her chemise, silk stockings, and flat leather pumps. All were ruined and beyond cleaning or repair.

Holly clasped the tub, stepping into the hot water, and a shiver stole up her spine. Warmth enclosed her as she sank down into the tub, a sigh of delight escaping her as the water lathed at her chilled, dirty skin.

"Would you like me to wash your hair now, my lady, or leave it until after I take these clothes down to the laundry?"

"After, thank you," she said, sinking into the water up to her chin, the warmth of the fire sprinkling a warm golden light about the room. How different tonight would be from the previous. To sleep in a bed, warm under a mountain of blankets, was something to look forward to after the trying few days.

A short time later, Jane returned, a handful of gowns and silk nightgowns folded over her arm. Holly turned to stare at the dresses. "Where did you get those from?" she asked, baffled.

"We had guests last week, my lady and the daughter of His Grace's guest, Miss Myrtle Landers, left these gowns behind. His Grace has given me leave to let you use them as it is unlikely that Miss Landers will be back to collect them."

Holly frowned. "Why would she not wish to have her dresses returned?" She picked up the soap and started to wash her arms, lathering her skin until a white, frothy foam covered her arms and hands.

"She eloped with a gentleman who was not her equal,

and so we shall probably not see her again," the maid said, cringing a little at the information.

"Well, that is indeed a reply I did not think you would give. Why was Miss Landers here?" she asked, curious about the woman.

Jane shifted on her feet, laying the silk undergarments on the bed. "His Grace, I believe, wished for Lord Balhannah to marry Miss Landers, but of course, that was before he knew of you, my lady."

Hmm. What an interesting tidbit of gossip. "Lord Balhannah did not know Miss Landers? Or were they well-acquainted?"

"Oh no, his lordship knew Miss Landers well. They spent much of their childhood here, I've been told. The duke and Miss Lander's father were close friends. It is believed that Miss Landers ran off and eloped. In her father's haste to follow his daughter, some of Miss Lander's things were left behind. I hope you do not mind wearing her gowns."

"Not at all," Holly assured the maid. The young woman in a neat black-and-white dress fussed about the room, placing more firewood on the fire and washing Holly's hair before leaving to give her more time alone.

Holly leaned back in the bath, closing her eyes. It was so very peaceful here, and lovely, the gardens were almost as beautiful as her own, or at least those that she'd seen on her arrival were.

Tomorrow, after she had written to Marco, she would ask Drew to take her about the grounds and down to the beach. If she had to stay here for several weeks, she needed to become acquainted with the lay of the land, see where she could hide if the worst happened here, or where she could flee if need be.

A tickle of movement skittered across her arm, and Holly stilled, opening her eyes to see a large, gray spider sitting on her flesh. Without heed, she screamed and stood, flicking the little beasty off across the room.

Footsteps sounded outside in the corridor before Drew burst into the room, a drying cloth about his waist and nothing else. She squealed, dipping back into the bath and covering herself with the water as best she could.

Drew ignored her nakedness and came up beside the bath, looking about the room. "What is it, Holly? Is there someone here?"

Her mouth dried as she glanced up at his back, still dripping with water from his bath. He had a lovely back, strong and straight, a small freckle just above the towel. She licked her lips. What would his skin feel like along his spine? Was it smooth and supple as it appeared? He was sunkissed there, not a pasty white like so many Englishmen, more in tune with her own people who spent a great deal of time outdoors.

"There is no one here, Drew. A spider landed on my arm, and I panicked. I've never been very fond of them."

He turned then, and his eyes widened before he spun back around, giving her his back. "Forgive me, Your Highness. I did not mean to look."

If words could sound like wincing, then Drew's most certainly did. She smiled at his unease, happy at least to be back in the bath where the soapy water gave her some means of modesty. "Have my maid come back and attend me and all shall be well. Thank you for coming to rescue me though. You were very quick."

He chuckled, the sound self-deprecating. "You're very welcome. I shall see you in our rooms shortly."

Holly stayed in the bath until her maid came back and

helped her out to dress. She changed into a silk shift and dressing gown that Miss Landers had left behind with little option. It was firm about her breasts, but otherwise fit her well. She and Miss Landers were of similar stature it would seem.

"There, my lady, you look beautiful." The maid smiled at Holly and walked to the door, opening it. "Shall I show you to the ducal apartments?"

Nerves skittered within her belly, and she clasped her stomach, the thought of being alone with Drew, to be sleeping in the same room, not because of circumstance or safety, but because of the charade they were playing, made it all the more concerning.

"Yes, thank you," she said, in a voice that was much more steady than her knees felt. "I'm ready to retire."

*D*rew paced the ducal rooms, waiting for Holly to arrive. Holy damnation, he had seen her naked and blast it all to hell if she wasn't as perfect as he thought she would be. A spider! A spider of all things had caused her to show the first crack in her armor, and blast and damn it if it didn't make her the most adorable being he'd ever beheld.

He went to the decanter of brandy his father kept in his old rooms and poured himself a glass. He would need all the fortification he could get after having the vision of her burned to the backs of his eyelids.

The sweep of her ass, the long-Meg legs that sat beneath that toned, rounded flesh. Her slim waist he'd wanted to sweep against his and revel in the feel of her skin. Drew swallowed, taking a calming breath. But it was her breasts that had undid him, neither large nor small, they were a lovely handful, and fell against her chest like teardrops.

He would never forget how perfect and sweet she looked, how her eyes were bright and large from fright, how she had not cared a morsel that he'd seen her naked... until she did.

Drew shook his head and went and sat on the daybed, running his hands through his hair. He needed to get a grip. She was not some heiress or debutante whom he'd saved from a rogue, much like himself, but a crown princess. A future queen who was well beyond his reach.

His eyes swept to the bed, mocking him that she was indeed out of his reach, but right at this moment, for several weeks would be well within his grasp. However was he to hide his growing attraction to this woman? To not slip and show her he would not revert to his rakehell ways and try to seduce her while she was here.

Holly trusted him, and he needed to ensure he never showed her how much her nearness, intelligent conversation, or perfect, generous lips made him want things he should not.

The door opened, and he stood, bowing. "My lady," he said, coming over to the door and closing it on the world beyond. He flicked the lock, hoping the lady's maid understood their need for privacy. In reality, he simply wanted to lock it and keep her as safe as he could. Not that a lock would keep out her uncle's men if they did storm Sotherton, but it would delay them a time.

"These are the ducal apartments. I hope you find it to your liking?"

Holly walked into the room, inspecting the bed that would be hers, the daybed, and roaring fire in the hearth.

She walked into the closet, and into the room beyond that was the bathing chamber.

She came back into the room, a small frown upon her brow. "Is there not an adjoining suite that your mother would have used? I only see where we're to bathe."

"My parents' marriage was a love match, and they did not sleep apart. Father had the room converted to a bathing chamber and the door to the passage is hidden from the outside. It looks like paneling on the wall. It is always locked and can only be opened from the inside."

"I do not remember my mother, but my father was fond of her from what he revealed during our childhood. She passed away at the birth of my youngest sister," Holly ventured.

"I'm sorry she is no longer with you. I should imagine you look very much like her?"

"Perhaps," she said, running her hand across the dark-purple velvet bedding. "Paintings would say I favor my father, but I do hope there is a little bit of my mother in my features."

"I'm sure there is." Drew waved the glass in his hand. "Would you like a brandy before bed?"

She raised one brow, sauntering over to him. "Do I scare you so much, my lord, that you require spirits?"

"Of course not," he lied, turning to pour her a drink before she noticed the heat that bloomed on his cheeks. What was it about this woman that made him nervous? She was royal, yes, but still, he was a lord, a future duke, they were not so far apart on the social sphere that she should make him a muddling mess, but she did. He supposed she was the first woman he enjoyed being around more than most and was forward, opinionated, and able.

All great qualities a man would look for in a wife, him certainly, but she was untouchable, forbidden to him.

Perhaps that was it.

Drew took a calming breath, throwing her a congenial smile, handing her the brandy. "To sleep," he toasted, "may tonight be much more agreeable than the last."

She smiled, clicking her glass to his. "That, my lord, is a toast worth celebrating."

He drank down the amber liquid, fighting not to take in her appearance. She was dressed for bed, the white silk shift and nightgown suited her, made her appear even more angelic than she had previously. A knot formed low in his gut as she finished her drink, walking to the bed. He could make out her form from behind, her perfect, pert ass and straight spine. Her long, chocolate locks he wanted to tangle his fingers through in passion.

He spun about, striding to the daybed. Without thought, he ripped the buttons on his breeches open and slid down his pants, leaving him only in his shirt. A small gasp, hardly audible, sounded behind him, and he realized that perhaps he ought to have remained clothed since they were unmarried and alone.

Instead of apologizing, he climbed onto the daybed, facing the bank of windows, the heavy brocade curtains pulled closed for the evening. "Goodnight, Holly," he said, staring at the curtains as if they would save him from himself and what he was starting to feel for this woman in his care.

"Goodnight, Drew," she whispered in a tired and throaty voice that sent his blood to pump. It reminded him of how his lovers had sounded after a good, thorough, satisfying romp.

The sooner she wrote to her guard in London and

procured a ship so he could take her back to Atharia and see her rightfully placed as queen, the better. To have her remain here would only lead to more trouble. Not of the violent kind that her uncle wrought, but that of the heart and that, Drew was certain, was trouble Holly was not looking for at all.

CHAPTER 10

*H*olly woke the following morning late, the sun already high in the sky. She sat up, her bedding strewn about the bed as if she'd kicked and turned all night. Not that she remembered doing so.

Her gaze automatically swung to the daybed. Disappointment stabbed at her, seeing it empty, the blankets Drew had used laid neatly over the end of her bed to hide the fact they had not slept in the same bed.

The smell of tea caught her senses, and she turned to look at the bedside cabinet, spying the hot, steaming brew. The staff here was very efficient.

Holly finished up her morning ablutions, with Jane's help. Not long after, she headed downstairs to find Drew. She found both the duke and Drew in the dining room having lunch. Both men stood, bowing at her arrival, and she came in, seating herself beside Drew. She supposed as his feigned wife that is what one ought to have done.

"Did you have a restful night, Holly?" the duke asked her, smiling in welcome. "Please bring Lady Balhannah her lunch."

Holly's stomach clenched with the reminder she had not eaten much over the past two days. A plate of cold meats and cheese was placed before her, along with another pot of tea. After their days on the road, the fresh bread, meats, and cheese were welcome. "May I have the use of your library, this afternoon, Your Grace? I have some correspondence that I need to attend to."

"Of course," he said, his eyes bright as he took her and Drew in. "I must congratulate you again on your marriage. It makes me very happy indeed to see my son so happily settled and with such a beautiful woman."

Drew cleared his throat, shifting on his chair, but didn't venture to say anything. Not that either of them could explain to the duke what was really going on under his roof. "I'm happy also," Holly said, not wholly untruthful with her words. The house was very comfortable, more so than Lord Bainbridge's, and the duke was pleasant, the staff more than accommodating.

"You mentioned that your family is related to Lord Bainbridge. Do you have an estate in England? Are your parents willing to come here and meet with us? I would like to welcome both you and your family to ours when you think they could attend."

Holly wished her parents could visit the duke. She supposed that she ought to keep to the truth as closely as possible if she had to lie to the gentleman. "Had they been able, I have no doubt they would have loved to have met you, Your Grace, and Drew also, but they cannot. They have both passed, my father early last year, my mother many years ago."

The duke slumped back in his chair, his eyes hooded with kindness. "I'm so very sorry, Holly. That must be very hard. Do you have any siblings?"

"I do, Your Grace. Two younger sisters." Holly forked a piece of ham and cheese into her mouth, savoring the taste.

"Very good indeed." The duke smiled at Drew, a mischievous light entering his eyes. "We shall have to find them both husbands at next year's Season. Drew is friends with many a gentleman who would suit most affably. Do you not think, my son?"

"I ah… Well, I'm sure Holly's sisters are more than capable of choosing their husbands, Father," he said, sipping from a small porcelain cup filled with coffee.

"That they are indeed," she ventured, replying to Drew's statement. "But if they do attend the Season, I'll be sure to use Drew's connections. Maybe there is a diamond amongst all the paste who would suit them well."

The duke laughed, and Drew threw her a curious stare. Holly smiled, shrugging. What did it hurt to play along with the duke's ideas for her sisters? Two women who were unlikely to ever step foot in England or take part in a Season. They were safe from Lord Balhannah's roguish friends.

"Now that you're married, my boy, I have had a thought. I need to have a painting commissioned of you both. The future Duke and Duchess of Sotherton. If only your mother were still here to see you settled so. It would warm her heart to know that you're happy."

Holly watched as Drew reached out, patting his father's hand that sat on the table. Although she had loved her father, there was little affection between them or either of her sisters. They had been brought up to be steadfast and strong-willed—future leaders. That did not mean she did not love them, she would, if need be, die for their future, but she had not had tactile parents. Seeing Drew comfort his father, even in this small way, left a longing inside her that she had not thought she would experience. When the time came, she would fight to be close to her children, be there for them whenever they needed her support, and show affection and love.

"I am happy, Father." Drew turned, throwing her a wicked smile. Her stomach clenched, and she could only feel sorry for the women who had fallen for such a handsome face. When he wished it, Drew could draw the water from the sea, she was sure. Devilish, handsome rogue.

They finished their meal, talking of nothing of consequence. Drew wished to inspect the grounds, ensure all was as it should be. No doubt to ensure her safety and well-being while she was here. If he kept treating her so well, she could very well end up staying here forever, for who in their right mind would walk away from such a man, such a life in the country?

A princess would. A future queen would.

Holly wrote the letter required to Marco after lunch, notifying him of her troubles at Lord Bainbridge's estate and her hasty retreat. Asking for word of Niccolo and if he had regrouped in town with the surviving men. Telling her guard to come to Lord Balhannah's estate via the sea and dock in the bay so she may travel to Atharia. There were only seven and a bit weeks left before her twenty-first birthday, and it would take some time for Marco to procure a vessel and sail it up the coast from London to the Suffolk county. By the time Marco arrived, it might be almost time for them to depart.

At least her uncle hadn't managed to hurt everyone at Lord Bainbridge's estate. One small mercy. Her next letter was to his lordship, letting him know of the troubles she encountered and that she would recompense his lordship for any repairs that were due after the attack. She also warned his lordship in the letter to be careful and not let Lady Mary out alone without his supervision, just in case her uncle tried to hit out at her through her friends.

She would not put it past her uncle to be so underhanded and cruel.

With the letters written, she sealed and placed the missives on the silver salver on the duke's desk. With her uncle's henchmen not knowing of her whereabouts, she would be safe here, and the post leaving the estate would not be intercepted. All would be well. She had to believe that.

Holly stood and started for the door just as a light knock alerted her to someone joining her. A smile slipped on her lips as Drew's handsome visage peeked about the wood. "Just the woman I wished to find. Would you care for a stroll about the grounds? You have been in here for quite some time."

"I would like that very much." Holly picked up her shawl she'd laid over a nearby chair and passed Drew, who held the door open for her. He strode up next to her, taking her arm and placing it on his.

His ease of touching her, of wanting to be near her, was so unlike what she was used to. Men, not even those of her station, dared not to pick up her arm and place it on theirs. Always correct protocol and etiquette were to be adhered to. It was nice to be treated like a lady whom his lordship may be courting in town. Not like a princess born to be queen.

They left the house via the front steps and started

walking up the long, gravel drive. Holly could hear the waves crashing against the shore in the distance, and the air had a distinctive scent of salt. Just as Lord Bainbridge's estate, Sotherton reminded her of her island home.

"Were you able to complete your correspondence?"

"I have done so, yes, thank you. Now I must wait to hear any news. I do hope it is better than what I fear. I am not certain what I shall do if Niccolo did not return to London and seek out his brother."

"If you have lost all those who are here to protect you and see you returned to Atharia to become queen, what shall you do?"

It was a question Holly had been asking herself for some days now. What if everyone she depended on was gone, dead, or injured? She bit her lip, tossing the thought about in her mind, hoping it would eventually make some sort of sense, a way forward.

"I could allow my uncle to take the throne, renounce my claim, abdicate."

Drew pulled her to a stop, watching her keenly. "Would you want to do something like that? If you abdicate and he passes away, you could not take the crown back, could you?"

"Uncle has no children, so my sister, Alessa would become queen, but it is not what I wish to do. I do not understand why or when my uncle became so cruel, but he must be stopped. If he can treat his family with such contempt and evilness, I shudder to think what he could do to the people. Those who do not have connections or wealth to protect themselves."

"You are more than welcome to live here, for as long as you need, Holly." Drew wrapped his hand over hers on his arm and started forward again. "I'm a selfish man for saying so, but I do enjoy having you here, and I'm not a man known for such sentiments."

"Really?" she asked, raising her brow, curious. "What kind of man are you usually, Lord Balhannah?"

"The type whom women call a rake."

She chuckled as he wiggled his brows at her. "Do you like to play with women, usually? Tease them into thinking that you love them more than you do before you discard them so cruelly?"

"Ah, nothing so bad as that, but I may steal a kiss or two. One thing I can attest to, however, is that I never dally with innocents. Of that you may be certain."

"That is very good to hear. I would hate for my husband to be a debauched rogue." His hand was warm over hers, and her stomach fluttered at his nearness. What would it be like to be kissed by such a man? To be his full attention, his wants, and needs.

"I have never been kissed," she admitted, staring ahead at the large oaks that lined the drive. "Women like me do not kiss men at balls and parties unless we want to start a diplomatic crisis."

"I would kiss you." His deep, gravelly voice halted her steps. Holly glanced up, meeting his blue, hooded gaze. His attention dipped to her lips, and she swallowed her fear. She knew upon speaking the words, of admitting just how innocent she was, that a little part of her hoped he would offer to take her first kiss.

The breath in her lungs seized as he dipped his head. "Last chance, Holly, before I kiss you."

She tipped her head back, raising her chin. His words, as low as they were, sounded like a challenge. As if he did not believe she would follow through on her subtle request. "I think I can survive a kiss from you, Drew. Men and women are supposed to kiss, after all."

"Yes, they are," he growled, closing the space between them and settling his lips on hers.

CHAPTER 11

*P*leasure thrummed through Drew's blood at his first taste of Holly. Never in his life had he felt such soft, supple lips. Lips that met his moved like a mirror image to his, and kissed him back with such sweet innocence that he ached. Holding her face between his palms, he deepened the kiss. Kept her locked in his embrace to savor the taste of her in his arms.

She was sweet, as he suspected she would be. He fought the urge to kiss her like he would kiss a lover, deep and thorough, wild and wanton. He was playing with fire kissing a woman so far above his reach. It was an absurd, crazy sort of thing to do. Nothing could come of them, he would marry a lady, and she would marry a prince. They could not marry each other.

Even so, when her hands settled over his shoulders, slipping to clasp the hair at his nape, the small thread of restraint holding him in place snapped.

Drew tilted her head and licked her bottom lip. She gasped, her eyes flying wide, staring at him in wonder. He took advantage of her surprise, kissing her soundly and tangling his tongue with hers. She let out a little sob of wonder, and his mind whirled.

What was she doing to him? Never had a kiss affected him so much. Already he could feel his hands shaking as he held her sweet face. He'd wanted to kiss her for days. Hell, perhaps even from the very first moment he'd laid eyes on her when she'd saved him, as foggy as that memory was.

She stepped into his hold, her body meeting his, and he was lost. He wound his arms around her back. Her breasts teased his chest through the silk of her gown. They were supple, her nipples pebbling through to graze his chest.

His cock rose to attention and he wrenched away, his breathing ragged. Drew stared at her, unsure of what had just happened, but certainly not ready to take that kiss any further. Holly's eyes were wide and cloudy with a lust he never thought to see. They had both been affected by that kiss, and what a kiss it was.

He took a calming breath, running his hand through his hair, a bark of laughter slipping from between his lips. "Well, Your Highness, how did you like your first kiss?" he asked, bringing them back to the point that it was only a kind gesture on his behalf to give her what she'd asked for.

She stared at him for what felt like an age before she said, "I fear that I shall never forget it, my lord. Quite satisfactory indeed."

He hoped she would not forget him, for he too would always remember kissing her. Drew rallied his shot nerves and gestured toward the path. "Shall we continue the tour?"

"Yes, lets," she said.

Drew glanced at her, not missing the unevenness of her

words. Silence settled between them, uncomfortable and strange, and he started to rattle off the names of the trees, the plants, and introducing her to the gardeners they came in contact with—anything but to bring up or discuss what had just passed between them.

He wasn't sure what that something was, but he wanted to do it again, by God. More even. She tempted him like no one else ever had. Her ease with the estate's staff showed Drew what type of woman she was to her people. She listened as Joe, their head gamekeeper, spoke of poachers and the number of pheasants he had under his care. Holly held the older man's eye during the short conversation, listened, and questioned him, proving she was engaged.

Drew doubted any lady of his acquaintance in London would care what the gamekeeper had to say. The women he knew may say they enjoy a stroll about the grounds, boating or horse riding, but sometimes he wondered if it were all a show—a play of words to merely get what they wanted—a duchess coronet.

Holly was in no need of his title or his wealth. She was a crown princess and beyond wealthy. Indeed a heady thing, he knew, for he was sought after in London due to who he was and what he was promised to inherit. Not because he was cared for at all.

They walked the grounds and stayed as close to the house as possible. Drew pointed to where the boundaries to his land lay. If he wanted to show her everything, they would have to travel by horseback, and at present, it was probably safer to remain close to the house and away from where others may see and recognize Holly from town.

"Ah, here you both are," his father said, meeting them

on the terrace as they walked up the large, flagstone steps, having finished the tour. "I had hoped to meet you here. Come indoors, there is a gentleman here to see you, Holly."

She cast a startled glance at Drew, and he went to stand beside her, clasping her hand. "What does he look like, Father?"

"Well," his father said, frowning. "Tall and muscular gentleman, dark-haired, bronzed skin, frowns a lot. He asked for Miss Holly Devereux. I, of course, corrected your name, my dear. No longer a miss but a marchioness."

"Thank you," Holly said, smiling a little at his father, who seemed oblivious to the underlying currents of unease running through them both. "We shall go indoors and meet with the gentleman."

They entered via the parlor and made their way to the library. Drew moved Holly to stand behind him as he opened the library door and sighed in relief when he recognized Niccolo's scowling face.

"Niccolo," Holly breathed, striding past Drew and up before her guard. "Whatever happened to you? Where is everyone?"

Niccolo flicked an annoyed glance at Drew when he closed the door but remained with them. "All are safe bar Lorenzo, who was killed. We have buried him on the Bainbridge grounds with a nice overlook to the lands. It has taken me some days to track you down. Why did you not wait for me at the shepherd's cottage?"

"We did wait, but we fled as we had no food and nothing to keep us warm. We could not wait any more than one night."

"And you thought to flee here?" Niccolo's words oozed

condescension, his narrowed eyes on Drew telling him everything he needed to know about the man. Niccolo did not like him and nor, by the looks of it, did he trust Holly in his care.

"Drew is Marquess Balhannah, future Duke Sotherton. I'm safe here with him and his father, the duke. We shall all be safe here until we leave for Atharia."

"We need to contact Marco and have him procure a ship and men."

"I have already done that," Holly said, walking about the desk and seating herself in his father's chair. Drew sat in the chair across from her, wondering if she even realized what she'd done. That without permission, she'd seated herself in a ducal chair, at his father's private desk where any manner of correspondence may be lying about.

He bit back a grin, admiring her strong, commanding spirit. She was a marvel and one he was utterly and unashamedly able to admit to liking very much.

Perhaps even too much.

"We do not know that this man did not bring your uncle to our doors, Your Highness. How do you know to trust him? Why even now," Niccolo said, throwing Drew a scathing glance, "they could be on their way here. Ready to wreak havoc and kill those who get in their way."

"Drew did not bring my uncle's men to our door. I know the reason why Lord Balhannah washed ashore on Lord Bainbridge's estate, and it is not because of my family. Please respect Lord Balhannah, Niccolo. He did not have to stay and keep me safe like he did. He could have fled and saved his own skin."

Unconvinced, Niccolo set his mouth into a displeased line, before he said, "Your birthday is in just over seven weeks. If Marco receives your missive by next week, we shall have the boat here within a fortnight. I suggest we set sail for Atharia, leave England while your uncle is still searching for you and believing you here. By the time we have arrived, your birthday will be imminent."

"What do you suggest I do upon my return? I cannot simply stroll into the palace and take the crown from my uncle's head."

Niccolo paced before the desk. The man was all muscle, oozed anger and strife, and yet even Drew could see how much he respected his future queen and would die fighting to keep her alive.

"The Medici family in the north of the island dislikes your uncle's rule. Reports you've read yourself state Alessandro Medici has been gaining support to overthrow the regent in favor of you, even before you come of age. We could travel to their estate, see if they would help us."

"The Medici's have often disagreed with the crown. I would not read too much into having their support."

"On the morning of the attack, word reached me regarding Princess Alessa. I was on my way to inform you of this news when we were attacked."

A cold chill swept down Drew's spine, and he steeled himself to hear what Niccolo had to say.

"What happened to Alessa?" Holly demanded, pinning her guard with wild, fearful eyes.

"Rumor in the court has been that the princess was being courted by Lord Wyatt Cecil, Earl Douglas, visiting from England."

"Wyatt was in Atharia?" Holly queried.

"Yes, Your Highness," Niccolo said, nodding slightly. "Your uncle was furious when he heard that Princess Alessa was favorable to his lordship's interest. He shamed her before the court, called her a whore for men's lust."

Holly gasped, her eyes bright with unshed tears. "And what became of Alessa after this shaming?"

Niccolo glanced out the window, seeming unable to hold Holly's eye. "He has thrown her out from all accounts. We do not know where she is. Reports state that he is now doing everything in his power to sully Princess Elena too. The court of your father's day is no more, there is no loyalty or etiquette or morals. They are out to ruin your family, and your uncle will stop at nothing to ensure he keeps the crown."

"He will pay for such cruelty. Poor Alessa, how she must be suffering."

"I know Lord Douglas, he's an honorable man. He will marry your sister if that is what is required for her reputation to be saved. If he were courting her, I should think that his intentions were noble."

"Like your own, my lord?"

Drew frowned up at Niccolo. "What is your point?" he asked, not liking the man's accusatory tone.

"I saw you this day, on the front drive, where anyone could have seen you, a commoner, kissing the Crown Princess. How dare you touch one hair on Her Highness's head?"

Drew stood, bringing himself eye level with the guard. "You may protect the princess, but you do not own her. She is her own woman with an independent mind. If she wishes to kiss me, I shall not refuse her."

Niccolo's eyes narrowed. "You are not worthy of her."

Drew stepped closer. "That is not for you to decide," he said, his voice hard with an edge of steel. He may not win a fight against this titan, but he'd give it a bloody good go before giving in.

"Enough," Holly said, her voice clipped and stern. "I

am here under the guise of Lord Balhannah's wife, Niccolo, and as such, I too must play my part. My actions here are my own, and for me to decide. Do not judge or interfere again. Do you understand?"

Niccolo bowed. "Of course, Your Highness. Forgive me."

Holly turned to Drew. "Do not argue with my guards, my lord. I do not need them to lose their patience with you and have your death on my conscience as well. My life at present is complicated enough without adding any more issues into it."

Drew sat back down, not entirely sure he liked being scolded like a boy. Even so, he could see Holly's point and would not aggravate the guard any further. They had a job to do, a plan to put into place, bickering between themselves solved nothing.

"We shall wait for Marco and the ship that will take me home. From there, we will travel to the Medici estate, secure men who will fight on my behalf, and engage my uncle."

"And what of him?" Niccolo threw out, his voice mocking. "He cannot come with us."

Drew narrowed his eyes on the man, his last nerve at the point of snapping with the fellow.

"Lord Balhannah has offered to help. He may be useful with the English noble families who are visiting Atharia. My uncle may be less inclined to start a conflict if there are people who will go back and report his actions to others in high society and royal circles."

Niccolo seemed to accept the explanation. Even so, Drew didn't give a shit what the man thought of him or his wanting to help keep Holly safe. He would see her returned home safely and crowned. If he were to do one thing in his life that was honorable, this would be it.

The duke strolled into the room, stopping when he saw the three of them, Holly behind the desk, her guard hovering over them all, and Drew seated. Drew could only imagine what his father was thinking. Who was this behemoth of a man who had come to stay here? And why was Holly seated behind his desk as if she were commanding an army?

Not too far from the truth, Drew mused.

"I do apologize, I thought you were finished in here, my dear."

"No, please stay, Your Grace." Holly stood, coming around the desk. Drew stood as well and stilled when she came over to him, wrapping her arm about his waist and holding him close. "Your Grace, may I introduce you to Niccolo, my manservant who was separated from us during our melee with the bandits. With your permission, I was hoping that you would allow him to stay for several days?"

The duke looked over Niccolo, his eyes widening the more he took in the man's stature. "Of course, you're welcome to stay. I shall have a room made up for you in the servants quarters."

Niccolo bowed. "Thank you, Your Grace, that is very kind."

"Nonsense," the duke said, waving the guard's concerns aside. "Whatever my new daughter-in-law wants or needs, we shall prevail to get it for her. Nothing is too much for our Holly."

Drew felt Holly stiffen in his arms. He glanced down at her, taking the opportunity to kiss her before her aggravating guard. She started at first, but soon melted against him, her hands clenched tight on the lapels of his coat when he deepened the kiss.

His father chuckled, and Drew was certain he heard Niccolo growl. Did the man want more from the princess than he was permitted? The thought gave him pause, and he broke the kiss, meeting the man's arctic, deadly stare over the top of Holly's head. Oh yes, he wanted more, and if murder had a face, Niccolo wore it.

CHAPTER 12

*T*he following day Holly walked down to the beach with Drew, looking out over the emerald sea, knowing that within a week or two, a ship would sail into the cove to take her home. That Drew wanted to come with her, help her, was an honorable gesture she was happy to receive, but it was also dangerous. Her future, her life back in Atharia, was uncertain, and to place others in danger, people who had no claim in her fight, seemed wrong.

"Drew, are you certain you wish to travel with me to Atharia? By doing so, you will be placing yourself in danger." To think of the man beside her being injured left a cavity in her soul. She did not wish to see anyone hurt. Drew was a gentleman, a man without too many cares. He could stay in England and live his life as if there was nothing to bother or naysay him.

His life with her would be complicated, and at some point, he would have to leave. The idea of that left a sour taste in her mouth. To think of him returning to England, of going on with his life without her, hurt, oddly enough. The unfairness of it all when he courted, married, and eventually had children with a woman who wasn't her.

She would not marry for love, but Drew could, and from the past few days having played his wife, the emotion coiling about inside her could be none other than jealousy. To be loved, kissed whenever one chose, touched, and conversed with without fear or reverence was a life she'd come to enjoy.

Wanted more of the same.

The waves crashed against the sand, reminding her of her location. "It is hot out today." Holly slipped off her slippers and carefully, without showing too much leg, pulled her stockings down, placing them in her boots. "Will you join me at the water's edge? I'm sure it will be refreshing."

Drew, who was lying beside her, one arm draped lazily over his eyes, sat up. "If you wish to." He kicked off his boots, discarding his stockings somewhere to his side. He stood, reaching down to her. "We can swim if you wish. Although it is a deep cove, it is shallow for some distance out."

"Oh no, I couldn't possibly." Even as Holly said the words, she liked the thought of the idea. She'd never been sea bathing before. She'd walked the shores of her home a million times, but to swim was not a pastime that a princess took part in.

"Whyever not? There is no one here to see you, and I shall keep you safe."

"I do not have anything to wear." She gestured to her light-pink muslin gown. "I will ruin one of the few dresses I have here at Sotherton."

"I shall send for more gowns for you." Drew pulled her toward the shore. "Come, live a little while you can. I'm sure such pastimes will be forbidden to you when you return home."

"Not forbidden, but certainly looked upon with disapproval." Holly took Drew's hand and walked toward the shore. The sand, warm under feet, tickled. The water washed up to her ankles and she laughed, jumping from the shock of the cold water.

"It is chillier than I thought it would be." She smiled up at Drew. "Are you certain it is safe to swim here? I have never tried before, you see."

"I will keep you safe," Drew said, staring out at the waves.

Holly held on to his hand, nerves fluttering in her stomach. Drew paused when the water hit his knees, letting go of her hand and pulling his shirt up over his head, throwing it back onto the shore.

Her mouth dried at the sight of him without a shirt. It had been two days since she'd seen him after his bath, but outside, the sun making his bronzed skin glisten, the muscles in his arms and stomach flexing as he walked and talked to her left her mind scattered.

Did he know of the effect he had on women? On her?

Holly tore her gaze away from the V that dipped beneath his tan breeches and studied the waves instead, jumping a little each time one rolled past them. The water lapped at her stomach, and she laughed, pushing down her gown when it bubbled up around her waist.

"I think this is deep enough," Drew said, dipping under the water fully and coming back up before her, running his hand through his hair and giving her a sinful grin.

Oh yes, the man knew the effect he had on women very well, and she was a fool to think otherwise.

Holly studied him, made no pains of taking in every part of his perfect self. How many women had this man been with? One or many, or, if she were lucky, none at all? She didn't like the idea of him being with anyone. Somehow in the past two days, she'd become a little green devil who wanted to keep this lord, her feigned husband, for herself.

A selfish action since he could never be hers.

She supposed she could have him as a lover once she married, but that wouldn't be fair, and she doubted her husband would appreciate the gesture.

A large wave crashed into them both, and Holly lost her footing, toppling over into the water. She fought to regain her feet, but her dress and the next wave halted her ability. Panic seized her that she would drown, leave her people at the mercy of her mad uncle before arms encircled her waist and hoisted her from the seabed.

She gasped for air, coughing, her hands gripped Drew's shoulders, the lifeline that he was.

"Holly! I'm sorry, I did not see that rogue wave."

She wiped the water from her face, blinking the stinging salt from her eyes. "I am well, thanks to you." Another wave rolled through them, and Holly noticed for the first time how far out they were, farther than she thought. She closed the space between them, wrapping her arms about his neck. "Thank you, Drew. You probably think me a fool for not knowing how to swim. A woman who grew up on an island and unable to swim seems a silly thing to be, doesn't it?"

"I could never think of you as foolish." His voice dipped to a deep, gravelly tone. Her breath hitched as if she were under the waves yet again. Her mind screamed to move away, have him help her to shore and dress, but she could not. Her heart had other ideas, and there was nowhere else she wanted to be but in his arms.

A wave pushed her against him, and her breasts grazed his chest. Goosebumps rose on her skin, his hands wrapped about her waist, holding her tight. Warmth speared between her legs, and for the first time in her life, her heart felt as if it would burst from her body.

Something was different today. Their closeness, the feel of his skin, the smoothness of the water left an ache low in her core. Holly bit her lip, meeting his gaze. He watched her, his attention fixed on her lips. Her pulse raced. Would he kiss her again? Oh, dear Lord, let him kiss her again. She wanted him with a burning need, both foreign and welcome at the same time.

Why not take what you want yourself? Why wait?

The thought flittered through her mind, and without further debate, she closed the last vestige of space between them and kissed him.

His mouth seized hers, and with a little nip, he teased her bottom lip. Holly gasped and Drew used the action to deepen the embrace, take her mouth, again and again, his tongue tangled with hers, sending her wits to spiral.

This kiss was different from their first. Raw and with an underlying need she too felt and wanted to sate. He kissed her as if the action kept him alive, a kiss of life, full of fire and need. With a boldness she did not know she possessed, Holly wrapped herself about him, linking her legs behind his back and kissed him. Her tongue tangled with his, hot and slick their mouths fought for control, for relief.

None came. If anything, the more they kissed, the

more she burned, her body alight and shuddering, aching for the man who held her hard against him. One of his hands dived into her hair, wrenching her closer. The action was bold, hard, and with an underlining demand that made her heart soar.

No one had ever kissed her this way. Held her captive and took what they wanted. What she wanted. She lost her breath when a growl of need reverberated from Drew. His kisses did not stop. He drank from her as she did him. Her fingernails scored his shoulders as heat licked at her skin, an ache at her core.

There was something that she wanted, but could not name. The more he kissed her in the sea, the waves rolling past them, oblivious to their surroundings, the more her body changed, came alive, yearned for another person, and not just any person, but Drew.

His hold increased, and his hand slipped to her bottom. With a lazy squeeze, he kneaded her backside. It was only then that Holly felt the hard line of his desire against the inside of her leg.

Had she done that to him?

A heady feeling came over her, and she undulated against his manhood, her core snug against his. She gasped and pulled back to stare at Drew when pleasure resulted from her brazenness. His eyes, hooded, blazing with heat, stared back. His chest rose and fell as if he'd run a mile.

"We should stop, Your Highness," he said, not letting her go despite his words.

Not that Holly wanted to go anywhere. She wanted more kisses from Drew, more of his touch. He was a distraction she hadn't known she needed before becoming the ruler of her people. The thought of letting him go, of marrying another man, a man of royal birth who did not raise the feelings and emotions that Drew did within her left her cold.

She shivered.

He started walking her back toward the shore, not letting her out of his arms. "You'll catch a chill. We shall return to the house."

She nodded, taking the opportunity to slide her hand through the hair at his nape, reveling in its softness. Once they made the beach, he set her down, stepping back.

"I do not know what this means, what is happening between us, but I find myself unable to deny you anything." Drew ran a hand across the back of his neck, holding it there.

Holly stared at him, uncertain what was happening either, but knowing she did not want what they had to end. He was the sweetest man she had ever met, and for the first time ever in her life, she felt alive. To be desired as a woman—not because she had been born with a crown atop her head—was an elixir she could become addicted to.

"Can we not simply enjoy what is happening between us and leave it at that, my lord? I do not need any more complications in my world. Being with you like this, kissing you whenever I like, is a little escape for me. Please do not take it away."

*D*rew stared down at Holly, knowing to the center of his core that he could not deduct anything from her life, certainly not himself. She made his heart sing, and his body burn, and he was loath to let any of it slip away.

He knew that their time would come to an end, but

he'd be buggered if he would let her go while he could delight in her world.

"I will acquiesce to your request, Your Highness. I will not ask anything more of you than you're willing to give." To take a step back from Holly, from how all his love affairs in the past had meted out was foreign and strange, but he needed to remember the woman before him was a virgin. An unmarried woman of royal birth. A crown princess for heaven's sake.

She could not dally with him, not while away her time in his bed and beneath him, no matter how much he may wish she could. She would return home soon, take her rightful place as queen and marry.

She smiled at his words, wrapping her arms about his neck, grinning. "You do not mind? I do like, you, Drew, very much, but I need you to understand that I cannot offer or promise you anything. I do not have the same freedoms as you do."

Drew pulled her close, wrapping her slight frame in his arms. "I understand. I shall take whatever you're willing to gift me. I will not push you for more." Even if the idea of leaving her in Atharia, to start a life without him, left an open, gaping wound where his heart currently sat.

"I suppose with us being as close as we are, our acting as newlyweds will not be so much a chore. I can kiss you whenever it pleases me."

Her sweet grin warmed his blood, and he reached up, pushing away wet hair that dared mar her angelic features. "And, I you," he whispered, leaning down and taking her lips. His body ached for her, his blood pumping fast in his veins.

This was dangerous. She was dangerous, and he ought to move aside, let her go, and not join her in Atharia.

Allow her to plan her attack without the added nuisance of a man falling about her skirts, but he could not walk away.

Drew ignored the warnings going off in his mind, thrust them aside, and kissed her soundly. He'd never played by the rules in any case. There was little reason to start doing so now.

CHAPTER 13

*T*he following evening after a delightful walk about the twilight gardens, Holly bathed and joined Drew in their room. Even though a devilish little part of her did desire seeing him shirtless once again, she knocked before entering. The thought of his golden skin, his muscular stomach that flexed with every breath, made her heart race.

He was becoming a little bit of an obsession that she needed to cure herself of.

All day she had found herself studying him, watching him as he read in the library, or how the wind played with his hair when they had walked about the gardens. Or how whenever he leaned down to kiss her, his eyes darkened with a determination that spiraled her wits.

How had she allowed herself to become entangled with Drew? It was beyond comprehension for a princess. The occasional dark looks from Niccolo reminded her that she was not acting like herself. That she had permitted her usually stone veneer to crack a little to let someone in. To be with the real Holly whom, like most women, longed to be loved and adored for who they were, not what they had. Drew was a rich, titled gentleman. He had no need to marry for wealth or situation. To know that he asked for nothing more than a few stolen kisses, of time with her, was a gift no one had ever given her before.

She walked to the bed, slipping off her robe and throwing it onto a nearby chair. Drew sat atop his, rubbing his neck as if it pained him.

"Is your neck paining you, Drew?" she asked, observing him like some obsessed debutante.

He glanced at her, letting the book he read slip from his lap. "I shall survive." He patted the space beside him. "Come here, Your Highness, I'm in need of my princess."

She grinned, going to him without question, slipping into his arms as if they had already been married for years, not days. And fraudulent days at that.

"Did you enjoy your bath?" he asked her, his hand idly rubbing along her side.

"I did, thank you." Holly turned, looking up at him. "You may sleep in my bed if you wish." Heat bloomed on her cheeks before she corrected her meaning. "I mean, you may sleep in the bed, to sleep, and nothing else. We have already slept so on our journey here, and I trust you not to attempt anything untoward."

He raised one brow, a wicked light entering his eyes. "You ought not to trust me. With such a sweet morsel beside me, I'm likely to take advantage."

Holly chuckled, shaking her head. "I do not believe that you would." Even though the idea of Drew touching her left her hot and aching in places she had not known even existed before he washed up into her life.

"I would not, no." He slipped down on the daybed a little more, pulling her into the crook of his arm. "You may sleep here with me if you choose. You're already here after all." Drew reached down, pulling the few blankets he had up over them both.

The daybed was comfortable and soft, and to have Drew beside her made it equally delightful. She lay her hand upon his stomach, idly playing with the muscles that flexed under the nightshirt he wore. "You're very toned for a lord. I had always imagined the English peerage as men who ordered people about and ate with an unappeasable gluttony."

"You would be thinking of King Henry the VIII, and I can assure you as a peer of the realm that not all English gentlemen are the same."

"You're nothing like King Henry and how very thankful I am of that fact." She continued to touch his stomach, being so bold as to move her hand farther on his person to the little V that she'd spied when he'd burst into her room during her bath.

Drew stilled beneath her, a small gasp fanning her face.

Holly glanced up. His eyes were closed, a small frown between his brows. Wickedness took hold, and she bit her lip, thinking of exploring him more. There was so very much to admire on his person, and if she did not take the opportunity now, she would forever regret her choice.

There would be no admiring Drew, touching and kissing him when he left her in Atharia. She would watch him sail away, and her little adventure, her heart as she had started to fear, would sail out over the horizon to never be seen again.

She looked back to where her hand slid over his lower abdomen. A woman would have to be blind not to see the jutting manhood. The pleasure made her lips twitch that he enjoyed her touch. A wicked curiosity tempted her to reach farther and touch him.

When they had been in the water the day before, it appeared as hard as steel. And yet, not in any way threatening. She'd wanted to purr against it like a cat and soothe the ache that thrummed between her legs.

Just as the throbbing was back now. She squeezed her legs together, being bolder than she ought and slid her hand down. She gasped at her first touch of him. Drew shook beneath her but did not try to halt her exploration. His manhood was hard, rigid, and jutted up toward his stomach.

No matter how rigid it seemed, it was covered in the softest skin she had ever felt. Softer than velvet or silk.

Astonishing!

"You're killing me, Holly," he moaned, his hand reaching out to the bedding beside him, flexing the sheet into his fist.

Excitement and boldness removed her caution. If she were to align her life with a man whom she did not love or find sexually alluring, at least she would have this moment. This night with Drew. Not that she would give herself to him fully, but lying here with him, touching him, giving him what she hoped was pleasure, was in itself pleasurable.

"Show me how to please you," she whispered, reaching up to lay soft kisses against his neck under his ear, his shoulder. He shivered, his hand wrapping about hers on his shaft and squeezing a little.

"Stroke me, slow or fast, it will not matter, just touch me, Holly." His words were strained, a deep, guttural sound that made her blood pump fast in her veins.

Holly did as he asked, stroking him, watching with amazement as it grew in size, thickened and lengthened, a dark-blue vein rising up its length, the head of his penis a deep, beautiful purple. He squirmed beneath her touch. Holly lay half on him, holding him in her hand as she fought to wrap her fingers around his length, stroke, and tease him. His breathing turned into pants, little puffs of air against her face.

She watched him, enthralled and delighted she could make him react so.

So this was giving pleasure...

Their gazes clashed, held, and she could not look away.

"Kiss me," he breathed, wrapping his hand about her nape and pulling her against him.

Holly would give him anything he wished, wanted to please and delight him in any way she could. A small part of her mind screamed that this was wrong, against the rules, not an action that a princess should partake in. If her family found out, she doubted they would ever look at her the same way again. As for her uncle, he would use it to tarnish her reputation, to out her to her people that she was not the type of leader to wear the crown.

No queen acted in such a base, derogatory manner.

Holly discarded all the thoughts as Drew thrust his tongue against hers, tangling, and teasing her mouth as much as she teased his manhood.

He moaned through the kiss, his rigid phallus hardened to the point it felt like steel. How was it even possible that a man and woman came together? That such a thing even fit within a woman's body?

The thought of Drew taking her, thrusting his penis into her aching core, made a gush of liquid desire to pool between her legs.

She wanted him to take her. Surely if men could gain

such pleasure from even the smallest act, a man could equally give a woman the same thing.

Drew gasped. "Harder, faster." His mouth took hers, punishing and wicked as she did as he asked. Warm liquid spilled over her hand, and she broke the kiss, determined to watch as he found his release.

He slumped back against the daybed, his breathing ragged, a small smile playing about his lips. "How unexpected and amazing you are, Holly." He reached up, running a finger across her cheek to slip over her bottom lip. "Let me do the same for you."

She bit her lip, uncertain if she should be so bold. If she allowed him to touch her so intimately, give her pleasure as she so obviously had to him, however was she to walk away? To leave Drew and step back into her royal role, marry a man who did not elicit such need and passion within her would be soul-crushing. It would be best that she did not. At least in this respect, she had to think of herself. Protect her heart.

There was no future with Drew, she reminded herself. No matter how much she had started to wish that was not the case.

"We best not. I should return to my bed."

He held her steadfast, refusing to let her go. "Do not leave. Sleep with me here."

Holly kissed him, pulling away and returning to her bed. She slipped under the covers, and despair swamped her. Much like her future marriage, the bed was cold and vacant. For a time, she watched through hooded lids as Drew cleaned himself before going back to his bed. Holly stared at the roof of her fourposter bed, the checkered linen pattern above her head.

She had a choice to make, one that would change her

forever. Not her path or her destiny, but her mind and body. For a woman who had always looked at problems rationally and without emotion, to have the dormant part of her body come alive, question the steps toward her future, question what she wanted, not for the country or her people, but herself, was difficult.

To have a heart that beat for another person in the world was as scary as it would be to stand before her uncle and fight him, and she wasn't sure she was strong enough to survive both.

If only she had not met Drew, she would not have this problem now. Her life would have one issue to tackle, and all would be well. Her gaze flicked to him, his golden locks all that she could see from this position, and her heart thumped hard in her chest.

Do not fall in love with him, Holly.

She cringed at her own thoughts, rolling over and thumping her pillow. No, she would not. She was a strong and independent woman, and she would not be ruled by anyone or anything, especially her emotions. That way led to weakness and demise, and if she were one thing in this world, it was not weak.

CHAPTER 14

The following afternoon Drew was almost in a panic and ready to call Niccolo when he'd been unable to find Holly. He had searched all the notable places within the home looking for her. The multiple galleries, billiards room, conservatory, the grand library, small library, chapel, lobby, and several servants' staircases along with the main one the family used were vacant of the woman who occupied his mind with alarming persistence of late.

He strode out on the terrace at the back of the house, looking out over the land. Where was she? A flash of color caught his eye, and he turned toward the large stone-and-glass greenhouse his mother had built the first year of her marriage and started in that direction.

The servants here wore black and gray, other than the liveried footmen. It was unlikely the color he spotted in the greenhouse could be anyone else but Holly.

He stepped into the glass-walled and glass-roofed building and slipped off his coat, sweat beading on his skin at the tropical temperature the plants within preferred.

He idled down a path, not wanting to look as desperate as he was to see her again. To ensure she was not offended by what had happened the night before. He needed to soothe his concerns that she would pull away from him, run from whatever was happening between them, and he'd never see her again.

Drew had a proper purchase on what was happening between them, and he could not sooner stop their course than he could stop the ocean from crashing onto the shore sands.

If he had to name what it was, he would say he was irrevocably, undeniably falling for the woman. A princess who was destined to be queen. A woman so far above his reach he would be a fool indeed to let himself feel anything other than respect and admiration.

Well then, he was a fool, for he could not feel those things and not feel everything else that came along with it. He adored her. Loved her, unlike anyone he'd ever loved before in his life.

Holly intoxicated his mind and soul, and he could not think of her leaving him, watching him sail back to England with her hundreds of miles away on foreign shores.

But how to make her see they were perfect for each other? No, he was not as wealthy as she, or of royal blood, but that did not mean that she could not love him despite those things. There was no set rule. Surely even in her homeland she could marry for love, marry whom she chooses, not what was best for the country.

He slowed his steps when he located her on a stone seat, her eyes were closed, and a small smile played about her lips. Was she enjoying the fragrant air that smelled of flowers, or was she thinking of him? He hoped it was the latter, but something told him she was simply enjoying the greenhouse.

He stepped on a small twig, and her eyes snapped open, meeting his gaze. She smiled, but the gesture did not reach her eyes, and he schooled the emotions that rioted inside him. "May I join you?" he asked.

She nodded, patting the bench beside her. "Of course. You're more than welcome."

Drew sat, staring out at the Hydrangeas before them, the tinkling sound of the fountain somewhere in the distance. "About last night, Holly. I wanted to check that you're not angry with me in any way. I should not have allowed things to progress as they did."

She looked up at him. He could see she was thinking over his words. Of what to say and how to get herself out of the trouble he'd brought into her life. He was a bastard, a fiend to have been so forward. He never should have allowed such liberties between them, and now that he had, just as he feared, he had alarmed her. Drove her away.

He started as she reached up, clasped his face in her hands, and kissed him. Drew moaned, pulling her close and deepening the embrace. Damn it, he wanted her, the fear of a moment before evaporating at her touch.

The kiss, sweet at first, soon dissembled into a hot, deep mating of mouths. His tongue tangled with hers, their upper bodies thrust together. Her breasts pushed into his chest, the beading of her nipples teasing his senses.

He wrenched her close, and a little purr of delight escaped her lips. He kissed it away, unable to get enough of her, be close enough. Sweat beaded his skin in the humid space, fragrance bombarded him, but still, the kiss went on, igniting a fire in his soul that he'd never experienced before.

Her green muslin gown was soft under his touch. He reached around, sliding his hand up her stomach to cover one breast. Desire gut-punched him, his cock standing to attention at the feel of her in his hands. Her breasts were generous, a perfect handful, and he kneaded the flesh, rolling one nipple between his thumb and forefinger.

"Oh, Drew," she gasped, thrusting farther into his hold. He teased her, wanting to give her as much pleasure as she had given him, not just last night, but from the moment they'd first met.

He broke away, placing small, teasing kisses down her neck. He took his time, savoring the sweet taste of her skin, the jasmine that rose from her hair.

"You're so delicious," he murmured.

Drew reached up and slipped the bodice of her dress down, exposing one breast to his view. He pulled back, the air in his lungs expelling at the sight of her bared naked to him. The word beautiful reverberated about in his mind like a drum, along with the word *mine*.

She was his, and God save his soul, he would do everything in his power to keep her with him. Even if that meant fighting against a royal protocol that said she should not marry an English gentleman.

He wanted the pliant, giving woman in his arms to be his. That, above all else, he knew to be. As true as the sun rose in the east and set in the west.

"Touch me, Drew."

He would give her whatever she wished. He dipped his head, her hands spiking into his hair, holding him against her as he flicked his tongue over her beaded, rosy nipple. The little nubbin crinkled farther, and he closed his mouth over her fully. She moaned his name, holding him against her. He took a calming breath through his nose, lest he lose himself in his breeches.

His cock ached and stood rigid, threatening to come out over the top of his pants. Still, he worked his tongue over her as if it were the lifeline keeping him tethered to this world.

Holly reached up, wrenching the other side of her gown down, exposing her other breast to his view. So beautiful, he sat back, both hands reaching out to touch her, revel in her gift. He wanted to hoist her on his lap, rip open his front falls and take her. Bring them both to fulfillment. Instead, he settled for loving her other breast, tantalizing her nipple with his tongue.

She tasted as sweet as a forbidden fruit. The sound of voices penetrated his hazy mind, and he wrenched back, looking past Holly to see who was coming toward them. Holly fought with her clothing, and Drew helped her back into her gown just as his father and Niccolo came along the graveled path.

"Holly, my dear," his father said, taking her hand and kissing it, "we have found you. Your manservant Niccolo has been in search of you. A letter I believe has arrived from Lady Mary."

Drew met Niccolo's gaze, annoyance thrumming through his veins at being interrupted from their delightful interlude. The man was starting to be troublesome.

"A letter, Your Hi—" Holly stilled beside him and Drew held his breath before Niccolo righted his words. "A letter has arrived for you, Lady Balhannah. It came via special messenger, and so I have been looking for you."

Holly stood, taking the missive before seating herself back beside Drew. "I was merely admiring the beautiful greenhouse of the duke. I shall be back inside presently. Thank you, Niccolo."

The guard bowed and, with one last narrowing of eyes on Drew, spun about and strode out of the garden.

"Your manservant is very protective of you, Holly," the duke remarked, staring after the man.

Holly nodded, breaking the seal on the missive. "He has been with me for many years and is perhaps a little overprotective, but that is his position, and he takes it very seriously."

"Perhaps a little too seriously," Drew's father said before he too took his leave.

Holly read over the letter before meeting Drew's gaze. "It is not from Lady Mary, but Marco. He has received my missive and without interference. He has procured a ship, and some of my men have survived," she gasped, smiling, throwing her arms about his neck.

Drew hugged her back, happy for her. "What else does the letter say?"

Holly read farther down the pages. "The ship will dock here in a fortnight where we shall sail to Atharia on the following high tide."

The pit of his stomach churned at the thought of Holly leaving England, not because he was unsure if she would ever return again, but because it meant she would have to face her uncle. Be placed in more danger than she was already in.

"How long will it take to reach Atharia?"

"A month at most." Her eyes read down the letter. "It is true that my sister has been exiled to Alessandro Medici's country estate. There is no news of Elena." Her mouth pursed into a displeased line. "I must return and fight for what is mine. Show my uncle that I am not afraid of him."

She studied him a moment before folding the letter and settling it into the pocket of her gown. "I will understand, Drew if you do not wish to accompany me. We are not married, going back to Atharia will mean that our time will not be our own, it will be different there for both of us. Are you certain you wish to help me? I have men trained for such circumstances to fight on my behalf. You do not need to put yourself into undue harm. I will not think any less of you if you do."

Drew wasn't ready to let her go, not now or ever. The trip to Atharia would take some weeks, and it would mean more time for him to spend with her. "You saved my life. I shall stay by your side until you no longer wish for me to be there. I will battle to ensure your future is secure and safe."

She reached up, touching his face. Drew leaned into her embrace, reveling in it. "You're a good man, Drew. Thank you for all that you've done for me."

He leaned forward, stealing a kiss, indulging in the fact she did not pull away, but leaned into his kiss, took her fill of him. "I have never been more thankful for a shipwreck in all my life, for it allowed me to meet you. I hope you know how much in awe of you I am. How much you confound and amaze me with your strength."

She grinned, a light blush stealing across her cheeks. "Do I really? How sweet you are."

"Yes, you do." And he was not sweet at all, merely a rake in love.

CHAPTER 15

Sotherton Estate, two weeks later.

*H*olly sat in the upstairs parlor the duke had given her for her own private use later that evening, a very annoyed and angry Niccolo staring at her from the settee across from her.

"He's a lord, a peer of England's realm, and you should not be dallying with him. You are the crown princess. You have Atharia to fight for, to defend against those who would take it from you. This guise as being someone's wife is as absurd as you or I marrying one day. An impossibility that you must come to see."

"I do see, Niccolo, and I do not need reminding of what is at stake in our homeland. I'm well aware of who and what is after my crown, but we're safe here at Sotherton, and if that means we have to play a game to return home safely and not have what happened at Lord Bainbridge's estate happen again, then I shall."

"Your uncle's henchmen have been seen at Stowmarket. If they hear of Lord Balhannah's new bride, they may come to see for themselves who one of London's notorious rakes settled with."

Notorious rake? Holly did not know what to make of that. "That would make little sense. Nothing is tying me to Drew's family or estate. They do not know what direction I traveled to after the raid unless you know something that I do not."

Niccolo's eyes went wide, and he shook his head. "Of course I do not. I know no more than you do, Your Highness."

Holly leaned back in her chair, watching her guard as he paced the desk before her. "I understand you promised my father upon his death that you would care for me, all of my sisters in fact, but you forget your place, Niccolo. I am the future queen of Atharia, and as such, it would be wise for no man to start chastising me for decisions I've had to make these past weeks. The circumstances are not what we planned, but having escaped and survived my uncle's attack, we are not doing so bad. You may not like Lord Balhannah, but he has kept me safe and given us the use of his home, he too is playing a game to ensure we leave for Atharia and can take up our roles in our homeland. Please remember those facts."

Niccolo stood at attention, a soldier to his core. "I do not dislike Lord Balhannah, but we know very little of him. I urge caution, Your Highness, that is all."

"I am cautious."

Niccolo scoffed, and Holly stood, her patience for the man coming to an end. "You disagree?" Her tone sent goosebumps over her skin. She did not like to act mighty and highhanded, but she would not allow her guards to mock her choices and question her morals.

"You have become very close to his lordship. If the

court was to find out that you have been sleeping in the same room as a man who is not your husband, I fear the repercussions."

"Who is going to tell the court this information, Niccolo? You? I have no one else here with me. My remaining guards are with Marco. It is only you who is here with me and knows the truth. Are you implying that if I do not behave, you will punish me with such degrading rumors?"

Niccolo blanched, shaking his head. Even so, Holly was no longer so certain about her guard's motives. What was happening here? He never questioned her choices. He'd always been steadfast in his resolve to support and protect her. She assumed the pressures they were under was the reason behind his cold demeanor these past weeks, but perhaps it was more than that.

Was he jealous of Drew?

"I am still a maid and intend to remain so until I marry. If I kiss Lord Balhannah, it is only so the staff does not talk of our indifferent marriage. It is so the duke does not find out that his son is harboring a woman on the run for her life. You will not have an opinion on this again, Niccolo, and I will not explain my motives to you a second time. Do you understand?"

A muscle flexed on Niccolo's temple, but he bowed and conceded. "I understand, Your Highness." Niccolo stormed from the room, the door slammed shut, putting paid to their conversation. Holly slumped onto her chair, letting out a relieved breath. Niccolo had never acted in such a way. Talking down to her as if she were a child in need of guidance. Of course, she needed opinions and support, but she was almost one and twenty, well past a girl in pigtails. She was a woman born to be queen, she was more than prepared for the role of ruler.

A light knock sounded on the door, and Drew popped his head around the threshold. His smile lifted her spirits, and she stood, going to him, wanting to be near his person. He gave her cheek a chaste kiss before placing her arm about his and leading her out of the room.

"I thought we could picnic for lunch today. A little north of the estate is a river. Our estate has a grotto there, and I thought you may want to see it."

She frowned, having never heard of such a place. "A grotto? Whatever sort of place is called such?"

Drew chuckled, grinning. "You will find out soon enough."

They took the curricle out to the private river that ran through the estate. A maid and footman awaited them, both standing a little from the grotto, setting up the picnic lunch they would have on the river's edge.

Drew gestured to the grotto his grandfather had found not long after becoming duke. It was a strange building, even one that Drew did not understand that well himself, but his mother had always loved the location, and therefore it would always hold a special place in Drew's heart.

"This is a grotto. Luckily ours is a naturally forming cave, but inside it has been changed to be more luxurious. Only the best for the Sotherton's," he teased.

Holly chuckled, stepping into the cave, her small gasp of delight warming his soul. He was glad she found it interesting enough to step inside. "What an amazing place. I never thought a cave could be so beautiful, and yet, this one is charming."

Drew joined her. "Being a natural cave, it is prone to flooding when the river runs high. That is why my mother had all the seats about the cave wall replaced with stone, the floors with large flagstones. It floods most winters, and yet it is always the same when we come to visit. I hope that my children and grandchildren can play in here as I did as a boy, and enjoy this naturally forming gift."

The footman came up to them, handing a glass of champagne to them both. "Lunch is prepared, my lord. Will you need us for anything further?" the servant asked.

Drew shook his head. "Thank you, no. You may return to the house." His servants did as he bade, and Drew helped Holly out of the cave and down toward where he'd had their picnic set up.

"I wanted to talk to you about Niccolo, Holly. I fear the man does not approve of my being near you, and after the glower he bestowed upon me leaving your sitting room this morning, I fear my take on the man is correct."

She sighed, taking his hand as she set herself down on the blanket. "He is against anything where I may injure or hurt my position socially. My being here, playing your wife, is not an easy concept for him to accept."

"Ah," Drew said, joining her on the blanket. "I thought he was jealous of me. Has it ever occurred to you that he may care for you more than a guard ought?"

Her silence was answer enough for Drew to know that the idea had crossed Holly's mind. "I spoke to him this morning. He understands what is at stake and why we're here. Niccolo will not cause any trouble."

"I'm not worried about that, I worry more for you. You can trust him, can you not?"

Holly glanced at him, her eyes wide with alarm. "Of course. Niccolo may be a lot of things—overprotective, famous in the royal court as a man who never stepped out of line, much to our lady's maid's annoyance. He does not like the situation we're in any more than I do, but we have little choice. He is merely going against all the rules he has ever followed by doing what I ask of him now. Once we return home, and everything goes back to how it should be, he shall return to rights."

Holly did not like the situation she was living? Drew looked out over the running water before him, an ache in his chest that she was eager to be gone, to leave his home forever. "We are not so bad to live with, I hope? I must admit to you, Holly, that when I return from Atharia I shall miss you. You are so very different from anyone I've ever met. I fear no woman shall ever rise to your level."

Drew downed his champagne, a lump the size of a ball in his throat. He was not sure where the overwhelming emotions were coming from. Why the idea of Holly leaving him to start her life where she belonged hurt and poked him in places that he'd not thought would ever feel anything.

Men of his ilk did not fall headlong in love with women. It just did not occur, and yet, the idea of Holly leaving, of not waking up next to her sweet face, of losing the smell of jasmine on his bedding, in his room, gave him the megrims.

She clasped his cheek, turning him to look at her. "I love it here, Drew. In the three weeks that I've been with you, as your wife," she chuckled, "I have never been more at ease or carefree." Holly placed her glass of champagne aside, lying beside him. "I shall miss this life when I return to mine. The situation is not ideal, but that is external to you. You have been a breath of fresh air that I did not know I needed to inhale."

Drew leaned down, kissing her. How could he not take anything and everything she was willing to give him? He was invested in her happiness and safety, and he never wanted to be parted from her. When he'd first offered to serve, he'd not thought anything further than assisting a woman in taking up her rightful place in the world.

How different it was now for him.

Now he never wanted to be parted from her side. She intoxicated his soul, and without her in his life, it would be a dull, stormy day instead of sunny and bright.

Holly clenched her fingers into his hair, pulling him close. She did not shy away from his kiss; she reveled in it, drank from him as much as he did her. The sweet melding of mouths soon changed to a conflagration of need, of promises and apologies for what could be. Her tongue tangled with his, her body rose up to press against his.

Drew rocked against her, and at some point, he was above her, settled between her legs. His hand wrenched up her gown to her waist, her skin as soft as the silk stockings on her legs. "I need to feel you."

She mewled beneath him, and his cock hardened. Holly helped him with her gown, rucking it up about her waist before she slipped one long limb over his hip, opening for him like a flower.

The breath in his lungs seized, but he had to feel her. He wanted to slide into her hot core, even if only with his fingers. Drew clasped and teased her thigh, electing an annoyed growl from Holly. Her heated skin burned his palm. He grazed his knuckles over her mons, the hairs on her cunny ticking his fingers.

With two fingers, he slid between her folds. Wet, so deliciously moist that his mind seized. She gasped, her hands scoring a line down his back. "Touch me, Drew," she begged.

Drew kissed her soundly as he moved to do as she asked. His fingers circled her aroused nubbin, paying homage to her sex before sliding farther into her heat. He wished he could shuck off his breeches, and make her his forever.

But he could not. This would have to suffice.

He teased her wet flesh, her juices coating his fingers, taunted, slid, and flicked her sex. If only they had more time, not just here and now, but always. He was sure he could make her fall in love with him, want to be with him forever. But with the boat arriving any day, his time was up. Soon she would be back in Atharia, and her life there would take precedence.

Holly broke the kiss, arching her back and gasping as the first contractions about his fingers took hold. Drew fucked her with his hand, giving her what she wanted as his thumb thrummed against her nubbin. She moaned his name, and the sound rocked him to his core, scared him in equal parts.

He had fallen for the writhing, loving woman beneath him, and he was powerless to stop it. That someone was trying to hurt her threatened to undo him completely. Never would he allow anything to injure her pure self.

Drew wrung out every last ounce of her pleasure he could before she slumped onto the picnic blanket, her eyes cloudy with desire.

"I never knew that being with a man could be like that," she said, staring at him with something akin to awe.

He chuckled, rolling beside her and pulling her into the crook of his arm. "That is only the beginning, my darling."

A small frown marred her brow, and he reached over,

wiping it away. He understood her concern, her fear and pain, for he felt it as well. "When we part, Holly, I will survive, I promise. No matter how much it will hurt to leave you, I know that we can never be any more than we are now."

Even so, Drew would do everything in his power to make that choice for Holly impossible to make. They were destined to be together. He'd washed up in her arms, for heaven's sake. If that was not fate, he did not know what was.

He would marry the woman in his arms or die trying. Life without her would be misery, and now that he'd found happiness, he was loath to lose it.

CHAPTER 16

*H*olly stood at the stone wall in the gardens and watched as the ship Marco procured them made anchor in the cove off the Sotherton estate. A small vessel came ashore, and four men jumped from the boat. Drew shook hands with them all, seemingly introducing himself.

They would leave tonight on high tide, much to Drew's father's protestations. Drew had made up the story that they were going to sail to the continent and enjoy the sights of Paris for several weeks. Although displeased at losing his son and new wife from under his roof, the duke did believe the trip would be an enjoyable time for them both.

If only that were true. The idea of returning to Atharia, facing her uncle, and taking up her rightful place as queen left a hollow feeling inside of Holly. To do all those things would mean she would lose Drew.

Her heart ached at the sight of him on the beach, the bottoms of his breeches getting wet as they loaded supplies and luggage into the small vessel on the shore. Marrying him in truth, of returning home as his wife had crossed her mind more than once these past days. Drew was from a powerful family. He may not be royal, but the alliance would be enough for her to make a stand against her uncle. What did it matter that all past crown princes and princesses of Atharia had only married into other royal circles? She did not have to do the same. If she did not, would it give her enough power to overthrow her uncle? Or would he use her choice against her?

Holly did not need to think twice about the answer to her question. Her uncle would, of course, use it against her. Tell the court and her people that she had married beneath her bloodline, placed the country at risk by the demeaning union. Her uncle had never cared for the English, and he would gleefully state that the Atharia royal line would forever be tainted.

No, she could not go against what her people expected of her. They needed a solid start to her rule, and a royal marriage would strengthen their homeland twofold. No matter how much she may wish Drew could bring such strength and connections, he did not.

Life was unfair no matter what creed or station one held. There were always situations that were not to one's liking.

Niccolo started making his way up the cove, heading toward her. "There are several more crates of food and water to be loaded, and then we shall be ready, Your Highness."

"Thank you, Niccolo." She did not look at her guard, their relationship since their heated conversation had soured a little. There was a distinctive chill in the air whenever he spoke to her that she did not appreciate. Very much unlike Niccolo and her relationship before meeting Drew.

"I must ask, Your Highness, if Lord Balhannah will be accompanying you to Atharia?"

She did look at him then, noting the muscle at his temple flexing as he awaited her reply. "Yes, he is." Holly refused to give any reason as to why. It was not her guard's choice how she went on. All that anyone need know was that she had saved Lord Balhannah's life, and he was returning the favor. To see her settled back in Atharia as the queen she was born to be.

"Very good, Your Highness. I shall make provisions for him in the vessel."

"He shall have a room beside mine, Niccolo. He will know no one and is there to protect me. Ensure my directions are followed."

Niccolo bowed, turning about and striding back toward the estate, his back straight as if a rod had been thrust up his spine.

Holly shook her head, turning back toward the beach to find Drew staring up at her, watching her conversation with her guard. From here, she could see the concern etched on his handsome face, and her heart flipped a little at his care. He'd gone above and beyond to make her feel safe and secure. He'd held her close while they huddled in the pit not far from Lord Bainbridge's estate on the night of her uncle's raid. From that night to this day, he had never left her side, nor did he try to make conflict with her guard. Niccolo, however, was going beyond his authority and creating issues where there ought to be none.

She would talk to her sisters when she returned home and decide who they would keep about them, who would remain in the palace to guard them. Niccolo, a man who had always had her back, always been loyal and supportive, was no longer so. Something was wrong, and it left her unsettled as to what.

He would never assume to be with her romantically, no matter what Drew may think, so then why was he so displeased? Holly raised her hand toward Drew, and he waved back, a small smile playing about his mouth.

The answer to her question contained a response that she did not want to face but would plan and prepare for in any case. She just hoped her greatest fear never eventuated and that she was wrong about Niccolo. That he was loyal to her and no one else.

*T*wo days later, they were sailing south on The Channel, England on one side and France the other. The day had been filled with meetings with Niccolo and Marco, ideas on where they would land and possibly allies they could count on once they reached Atharia. As agreed, they would sail to the north end of the island and anchor off Medici land. They were a powerful family and one who had made a public declaration against her uncle. Not to mention that her sister currently resided under their roof. They would be an ally, she was sure of it.

Holly looked forward to seeing Alessa again. Once she knew her sibling was safe and well, she would go about getting Elena out of the palace. Then and only then would she strike out at her uncle and make him pay for all that he'd done against her and their family.

She started toward her cabin, smiling at the sight of Drew trying to gain his sea legs. He was not the most stable of gentlemen she'd ever beheld on a ship, and his inability to stay upright had become a bit of amusement for the crew and for her.

Holly knew she should not laugh at him, and of course, eventually, he would become steady, but it was a little amusing to see him stumble at the slightest rock of the ship.

"Can I help you to your cabin, my lord?" she asked, coming up behind him and wrapping her arm about his back. The last two nights, they had not slept in the same room, and strangely she had endured two of the worst night's sleep of her life. The bed was uncomfortable, the room did not smell right, and the mere fact she was alone in the dark without a man she trusted more than she ought considering she had not known him very long, left her discombobulated.

"Please." He chuckled ruefully. "One would think I would be capable on a ship, but here you are, I am not. I am but a mortal man after all and one who does not have sea legs like yourself."

"I have traveled by ship all my life. You too will gain your sea legs, my lord. You will have four weeks to grow them."

He leaned close, his whisky-laced breath doing odd things to her senses. Her skin prickled in awareness, and she wanted to lean into him, make their closeness last forever. "I have missed you these past nights. Tell me you miss me too."

She glanced at him sharply, having not expected him to be so bold, not here on a ship where anyone may overhear his words. "You tease, my lord."

They made the stairs leading down toward the cabin, and Holly helped Drew down them before starting toward his room. "I'm not teasing at all, now answer the question, Your Highness, and prove me wrong."

She shrugged, standing before him. "Of course I have

missed you," she whispered, but it is what it is. A situation we both must endure."

"Really?" He cocked one brow, reaching for a door handle at his right to steady himself. "Have you seen my rooms, Your Highness? They are very spacious and luxurious."

Holly strode past Drew and swung his door wide, walking into his room that was the size of one of her maid's closets back in Atharia. One could not twirl a cat in such a space. She turned, watching as he closed the door, slumping against it. "I cannot stay here with you. You know I cannot."

He ran a hand through his hair, leaving it on end. He looked disheveled and too handsome for his own wellbeing. Drew was a complication, a gift she had not thought to come across while in England. She'd traveled to the country to simply enjoy one of the *ton's* famous Seasons in London. She had not thought to meet a man who encompassed all she looked for in a husband and want him desperately.

The idea of throwing herself at him in his cabin made her body ache with a need that frightened her. Would she always long for this man as she did right at this moment, or was it merely a passing fancy? An emotion that women could have with any man if they chose to?

That she did not know, but what she did know was that she could not leave this room without one stolen kiss from his lips. She closed the space between them, kissed him hard, took what she wanted with no regrets and no thought of the consequences.

Drew wrapped his arms about her back, pushing her up against the side of the cabin. Her bottom knocked against the small writing desk that the room housed, and without wavering, Drew hoisted her atop it, settling between her legs.

Heat pooled at her core. Hot and wet and thrumming with need. She wanted him to touch her, make her find the pleasure he brought her only days ago.

"Let me make you come. I promise that you'll remain a maid. Will you let me?" he asked, his eyes wild with a need that spiked her own.

She nodded, wondering what other wicked things he knew.

Drew pulled back, hoisting up her gown to pool at her waist. Cool air kissed her thighs and heat bloomed on her cheeks, expectation thrummed through her veins like a drum at the thought of what he would do to her. He pushed her legs wide, and she watched as he licked his lips at the sight of her mons.

Holly swallowed, clasping the desk as he tore his gaze away to his breeches, wrenching open his front falls. His manhood sprung free, and she reminded herself he'd promised to keep her a maid. She took a calming breath, trusting him to hold his word.

He took himself in hand, squeezing along his length, a small, pearly white bead of his desire settling on the top of his penis. Her core ached. For the first time in her life, she could understand why a woman desired a man to take her. To thrust that hard rod inside of her heat to soothe the unrelenting need pulsating there.

"Trust me," he whispered, kissing her soundly as he wrenched her forward on the desk, placing her core hard up against his manhood. He thrust against her, running the velvet-enclosed steel along her slick heat. Holly gasped, wrapping her legs about his back, pushing herself against him. Wanting to feel the sensation of him. Needing him to bring her to the pleasure she craved.

Her skin burned, her heart thumped fast in her chest. It wasn't enough. She wanted more. More of Drew and what he could give her. Her mind cautioned her, warned her against such a bold and reckless action. Holly reined in her desire, settling for what he could give her here and now, that would leave her a maid.

"So sweet. I want you so much," he gasped against her lips.

I want you too, Drew, more than you'll ever know. "You make me want things I cannot have."

He threw her a wicked grin that sent her wits spiraling. "I want to make you moan my name every day. I want to kiss your sweet lips here," he said, the brush of his lips featherlight and not enough. "I want to kiss your lips here." He ground against her, teasing her to the point that she did not know how she would survive. It was too much and yet not enough. Never enough. "I want to lick you until you ride my face until you fuck me, take from me your pleasure, over and over again. I want to watch as you arch your back in climax. I want to watch you as I fuck you hard and fast. I want to do all these things to you."

She kissed him deeply, scoring her nails down his back as her body came apart. Pleasure burst through her like a light. Her core convulsed to the point of pain, and still, he ground against her, wringing from her all that he could.

Holly fought to breathe. To stop herself from shouting his name. He moaned against her lips, kissing away her gasps. Warm liquid spilled against her mons, over the thatch of curls between her legs. Drew shuddered against her, her name a chant repeated over and over again.

They stayed like that for some time, joined together in

pleasure, and not willing to let each other go. Holly doubted she would ever be ready to see Drew leave, to move on with his life back in London with a respectable English woman of his class.

"Stay with me tonight," he begged, reaching beside him for a towel. He stepped back and wiped her sex, cleaning her up as best he could. She allowed him the liberty, enjoying his touch there. She was scandalous to allow him such freedoms with her body, but she could not help herself. At some point, she had grown to adore the man taking great pains in wiping her aroused flesh. She would not deny him anything.

"You know that I cannot. The men on this ship are from my country, and I do not need them knowing of my attachment to you."

He grinned, pulling her skirts back to settle about her ankles. "You have an attachment to me?" he teased, sliding one finger under her chin and raising her eyes to look at him.

Holly saw no reason not to be honest. "You know that I do."

"That is very welcome news, Your Highness, for I have an attachment toward you also, and one I'm loath to walk away from."

Did Drew mean he would fight to stay by her side, even knowing there was no future between them? She could not allow him to do so. He must leave, return to England and have a full and happy life in his homeland. She would not let him stand by in Atharia and watch as she married another, gave her body to another man. She, too, could not do such a thing to her own heart. If she were to marry another, have a future without Drew, she did not need him in Atharia, tempting her away with every look, every stolen touch.

She chuckled, making light of his comment. "And yet I must before someone catches me in your room." She slipped off the desk, leaning up for one more kiss. His mouth took hers, and she fought not to lose herself in his passion.

It would be so very easy to fall so hard that one could never pick themselves up again.

"Good night, my lord," she said, turning for the door.

Drew leaned up against the wall, idly tying his front falls back up. "Good night, Holly."

She sighed, forcing her feet to move out of his room and away from the delectable sight he made, all rumpled, a little tipsy, his dark, hooded eyes promising more sin and seduction. An impossible man to deny oneself. However was she to survive the trip to Atharia with Drew tempting her at every turn? As she shut the door to her own room, she knew she could not.

She'd already failed.

CHAPTER 17

*D*rew watched from afar as Holly and her two guards, blood brothers, Niccolo and Marco spoke at the bow of the ship, their frowns of worry etched on their faces making dread coil in his blood.

They had been sailing toward Atharia for over three weeks now. Some of the best days of his life if he were honest. Holly stole into his cabin each night, their interludes becoming more and more erotic, longer and harder to resist. He was now in a constant state of arousal.

They had laid out on the deck at night, watching the stars and trying to navigate via the constellations. They had played chess and cards, ate with the crew, and enjoyed dancing and singing on the nights the crew had brought out their musical talents.

The time on the ship had passed in a blink, and soon they would have to face Holly's future and the man who strove to take it away from her and her siblings.

From here, he could see the armed guards standing on the docks of one of Holly's kinsmen, the rich and powerful Medici family where her sister was supposedly taking refuge. The men looked like an army of three hundred, ready for battle. It did not bode well for their plan to stay at the estate.

Holly dismissed her guards and turned, walking down the ship's bow toward where Drew waited for her. "We shall dock and hope they allow us the time to explain who we are. We cannot sail my royal standard, for we do not wish to alert my uncle if he has men watching the area. I have little doubt that he does so."

"Do you believe it is safe to dock there? What if they attack?"

"My men are preparing now. Marco has his own men who work for him. They are as well-trained as my own. Nothing shall happen to us, Drew."

"Nothing will happen to you, for you'll be locked in your cabin. I shall be out here with the men, protecting you." He did not even want to think about Holly being cut down, slaughtered by madmen. To lose her would send him into a spiral of retribution, and he would not rest until all of those who did her harm paid for it with their lives.

"There will be one among the Medici guards who know me. I must be visible so we can all remain safe and be allowed us to pass." She reached out, clasping his arm. "All will be well, Drew. Do not worry so." She grinned and pushed past him, heading toward her cabin.

Drew let her go, watching as they came nearer to the docks, the armed men and their scowling, vacant, emotionless eyes less than welcoming.

Their ship drew up against the dock, and thankfully, the guards ashore allowed their crew to tie the boat secure.

Holly stepped into view, and the men, their faces hard and unforgiving, changed as quick as the wind. Shock registered on their visages before they knelt in unison, placing their swords against their chest. One man stood, bowing his head as he spoke. "Your Highness, forgive our cold welcome. We did not know who you were."

Holly took Drew's hand as he helped her step onto the dock, Niccolo and Marco close on her heels. Drew placed his hand on the sword he was given for use in an "in case the worst happened" moment, and he was not shy of using it.

"No offense taken, General. Please take me to Alessandro if you will."

"Of course, Your Highness," the general said, leading them past the armed men who remained bowed in respect. Uneasiness slid up Drew's back at the reverence with which they treated Holly. They respected and cared for this woman as much as they did their country.

To see such deference was humbling and not a little unnerving.

He'd grown so very close to Holly over the past weeks that he'd forgotten at times who she was. To him, he'd treated her as a woman of independent thought and capabilities, of charm and someone who made him laugh more than he ever had in his life. She was a breath of fresh air, and he was reluctant to lose her. Holly was a woman to him, his lover, but not a future queen, or crown princess.

Seeing her here and now, the way the people looked to her for strength told him more than anything that their time was coming to an end.

She had responsibilities here that were insurmountable and well beyond his schooling. All her life Holly would have been trained, taught and schooled into being a leader, a queen. He'd been schooled, yes, but after Cambridge, he'd spent his time in London, multiple follies and affairs with women, biding his time until he was forced into a loveless marriage.

That he would find a woman who would actually persuade him into the commitment wasn't something he'd bargained for. Having Holly taken away from him because he wasn't of royal blood made his stomach churn.

They entered the white stone villa surrounded by a large stone wall to stop anyone not invited to gain entrance. The house was a grand representation of wealth and Roman architecture. Windows glistened that overlooked the Mediterranean sea. A warm breeze floated through the house, and a group of servants stood beside the front door, lined up in welcome.

A woman rushed down the central staircase, her long, golden locks bouncing down her back and shoulders. She cried Holly's name, and before anyone could stop her, Holly had darted forward, wrapping her arms about the woman, holding her tight.

Drew stood back, watching as Holly gushed over the lady she called Alessa in her arms. They were similar in height and form and together made a striking pair. Drew could only wonder if the third sister Elena was with them and looked just as remarkable. The three princesses would be the envy of anyone.

A tall, older gentleman with graying hair joined their party and bowed. "Your Highness, welcome to the Medici estate. You and your party are most welcome here. Come inside, and we shall have refreshments and discuss your situation further."

"Thank you, *Signore* Medici. That is very kind of you." Holly took her sister's arm, letting her sibling lead them toward the stairs.

The house was laid out much like a Roman home, tiled

floors, large, open spaces, water features, and murals on the walls. They headed upstairs and into a large room that overlooked the ocean, the windows open, the sheer, almost transparent curtains billowing into the room.

Drew kept to the rear of the group, not wishing to impose on the conversation or what Holly had to discuss with *Signore* Medici. This was her land, her people, and she would know best how to go forward, although a little part of him wished she would reach for him and ask him for guidance. He may not know exactly what to do, but he could try.

As the conversations started, Niccolo and Marco sat on either side of Holly and Alessa, two solid masses of muscle and protection, immovable and strong. In all the time he'd known Holly, this was the first that Drew felt like an outsider and irrelevant. He swallowed, steeling himself to feel such for some weeks yet to come.

*H*olly listened as *Signore* Medici spoke of how he was at court, and it was then he noticed that Alessa and Elena were being denied their rightful place during entertainments and dinners. "He was keeping them locked up, separate from the people who attended to see them. Of course, I did not know this at the time. It was revealed later when my son overheard two servant girls talking of the princesses being held in their room and refused any requests they may have."

Anger thrummed through Holly's veins at the gall of her uncle to treat her siblings so. The future Queen of Atharia's sisters did not have their place, their position at court denied them by a second son who was never going to be king.

How dare he.

"And Elena is still at the palace. How did you become separated?"

"That was Elena's idea, Holly," Alessa said. "She wanted me to get word to you somehow, to our friends. I bribed a footman and was able to sneak over to the guest wing of the palace. I spoke with Soren Medici, and he notified his father of our plight. We left that evening under cover of darkness. Elena knew that should the opportunity arise, I would leave. She is safe from all accounts but still denied the ability to leave her quarters. Uncle must be stopped, Holly. The way he treats our servants and his disdain and loathing he does not disguise when talking to the people sicken me."

"I understand," Holly said, her mind whirling with plans and how to enact them. "The royal house of Atharia is still in court. There are many families in the palace. We need to return to the city, arrive with a full procession, let the people know that I have returned, let them see you and I enter the palace. In front of the peerage and royal family, Uncle would not dare deny us. But if he does, we'll know how to act."

"What will you do if he denounces you?" Niccolo asked, a deep furrow of concern etched on his brow.

"Show my hand," she answered without caution. "I will strike at anyone who dares to hurt my family or me." Holly looked over her two guards, her sister and *Signore* Medici, who stood listening with a bevy of his own armed men. "It will not only be Alessa who arrives and me but an army of men. Many men loyal to me and my father's bloodline, the rightful heirs to the crown. You all shall be standing behind me, noble families all. We need the numbers to outman my uncle and the few cronies who follow him. The palace has over two hundred and fifty guards. We need more than that. Let Uncle see our strength and let him do as he will. I will not allow him to best me or take away what is mine by birthright."

"With that, I hope *Signore* Medici, Soren, and myself have been helpful to you, Holly," Alessa said, taking her hand. "We have been gathering men, seeking help to overthrow Uncle. We have close to a thousand men who are willing to fight in your name and Atharia."

The news sent relief to spiral through her. Her sister could not have given better word. "Let us hope we do not need to have a physical war with Uncle, but at least we will be ready should he not step aside peacefully." Her uncle was not a kind man. Fighting him meant she would make a lot of enemies. Even so, it was worth the risk.

Holly glanced over her shoulder, seeking out Drew. She had not seen him much during the conversations, but she would welcome his input and support. Not seeing him, she turned back to the conversation.

"Uncle may strike out and harm Elena. We cannot allow that to happen. He must not know of our coming to court. With us there, he wouldn't dare hurt her." Alessa squeezed her hand before meeting Soren Medici's eye. Something passed between the two of them. A flicker only, no words spoken, but the younger Medici seemed to understand her sister's bidding and clapped his father's shoulder. "Come, Father, everyone, we shall return to the library downstairs and discuss matters further. Give Her Royal Highness and Princess Alessa some privacy."

Signore Medici's eyes went wide but seemingly understood the sisters needed solitude. "Of course, yes. We shall leave you now. Join us downstairs at your leisure."

The men slowly made their way out of the room. Holly

watched them go, looking for Drew again and unable to locate him. She sat beside Alessa, happy to be back in Atharia and with her sibling once again. She would find Drew soon and see where he disappeared to.

"I'm so very glad that you're home, Holly. I have missed you dreadfully, and now with Elena in trouble, I was starting to think that I too would have to flee Atharia to remain safe."

"Nowhere is safe. Uncle tried to rid me of this world in London. It was how I ended up at a country estate with Lord Balhannah."

"Where you met your handsome Englishman." Alessa grinned, reminiscent of how she used to look before their father died, and their uncle had become a madman.

"One day, I shall tell you the whole story of how we met." Heat rushed onto Holly's cheeks, and she shook her head at the fact she was a little lost for words. A little discombobulated whenever Drew was around or in her mind.

"What do you think of Lord Balhannah?" Holly asked, curious to hear what Alessa had to say.

"So many things that I think, but the one most of all is how you managed to get him to look at you the way he does. Even just before, downstairs, when I greeted you, his affection was evident. When he was standing against the wall during our meeting, he watched you, listened to you talk as if you were the smartest, most rational mind here, His lordship had the oddest expression on his face."

"What sort of expression?" she asked, missing Drew already, and she had only been separated from him for a few minutes. However was she going to survive when he returned to England? When she stepped forward in life, married another, and ruled here?

The nightmare wasn't worth thinking over.

"I do not care if you disagree, or try to persuade me otherwise, but Lord Balhannah is in love with you. It is written on his face as clear as his golden locks are on top of his head. What are your thoughts on this? Does this mean our eldest sister has come around to the idea of marrying for love? Has disregarded seeing marriage only as a duty and alliance building for Atharia?"

"You know that I do not have that freedom, even if I wanted to marry him, or loved him, it is not possible. Lord Balhannah will return to London, and I shall continue on here."

Her sister threw her a disbelieving look, wagging her finger before her face. "Oh no you do not, Your Highness. I've never seen your eyes glass over the way they just did when you mentioned his name. You love this man too. Have you told him that you do? I hope you're prepared to tell our advisors back at court that it is your life, and as queen, you may marry whomever you please."

Holly stood, striding to the window to gaze out over the ocean. "That is just it, Alessa, I cannot do that. It has proven more than ever that my marriage must be one of power and influence with Uncle's threat. Drew may be a marquess, a future duke even, but he is not royal. I must marry into a family of strength, a family that rules over countries, not counties."

Alessa joined her at the window, taking a moment to look out over the ocean as well. "Stuff and nonsense, you have to do anything. Father did not think you needed to put your own happiness before that of Atharia. I certainly will not, and neither will Elena. Our people love you. They do not want to see you in a union that makes you unhappy. You deserve more than that."

Holly blinked the tears that blurred her vision. She wished what Alessa said were true, but it was not, nor could it ever be. Her situation was different, no matter how much her sisters may wish it otherwise. It was enough for Holly to know that at least Alessa and Elena could marry for love.

"I adore Drew, he saved my life back in England, and I will forever hold a special place for him in my heart, but he knows and understands that there is no future between us. You, too, need to accept this."

Holly turned from the window, striding for the door and ignoring Alessa's calls for her to stop. She could not talk about this situation any further. To do so wrenched a hole in her chest where her heart was supposed to beat. She made her way up the corridor, a maid beside a door bobbing a quick curtsy.

"Your Highness, your rooms are ready if you would like to rest for a time."

The maid's words were like a gift, and she nodded, hoping the servant did not notice her upset. Within a minute, she was led into a spacious room, whitewashed walls, and furniture, a striking dark-blue bed coverlet, and curtains suited the house's location.

"May I assist you with anything, Your Highness?" the young woman asked, standing with head bowed and hands clasped at her front.

"No, thank you. I wish for solitude."

She dipped into a curtsy and left without nary a sound. Holly walked over to the bed and threw herself facedown atop the bedding. There was so much to do. They needed to leave for Atharia, and moving over a thousand people without being seen would not be an easy feat. Her uncle was no fool. He would find out, and then there would be trouble.

Holly rolled over, staring up at the ceiling that was engraved with a variety of designs. She had never been one to give up, to accept defeat with anything she did in life, but perhaps this was a time she needed to step away, let her uncle have his kingdom. The thought made her shudder, and she knew she could not do that, no matter if her heart and mind were at war over the decision.

To win her kingdom would mean she would lose something else that had grown just as important to her.

Drew.

CHAPTER 18

It wasn't until the following evening that Drew was able to have a moment alone with Holly. All day she had been discussing plans, sending men who were loyal to her toward the capital of Atharia, where her uncle resided in the palace.

They had decided to gather the men there in the city throughout a couple of weeks, instead of in one large march into the city. Some of the aristocratic families were already in place, waiting to support Holly. The atmosphere here where they were staying, however, was not to Drew's liking. He had the distinct feeling none of the Atharia people who rallied around Holly cared for his presence, so much so that yesterday he'd stayed in his small room and kept out of everyone's way, notably Holly's. He did not wish to cause her any more concern or difficulty than she was already dealing with.

Dinner this evening had seen him placed at the opposite end of the table to her. She had not glanced in his direction once, and he disliked the emotion it brought forth within him. He'd seen her speaking to the dashing Soren

Medici, heir to this property, and had noted how he'd gazed at her in reverence. Drew had thought the young man had feelings for Holly's younger sister, but perhaps he'd been wrong in that estimation, watching the gentleman even now fawn all over the woman he wanted like his lungs needed air.

"If you wish to keep her, Lord Balhannah, you will need to fight and perhaps even a little dirty as well. She's the future Queen of Atharia. She was not brought up to marry anyone other than her royal equal. You will need to change her mind about that."

Drew started at the sound of Alessa, who came to stand beside him. He glanced at her, her long, golden locks coiled high upon her head this evening, a decorative diamond-encrusted tiara on her head, making her look the perfect princess. Holly too this evening was adorned in jewels and a regal, dark-purple evening gown that made her eyes sparkle. He'd lost his breath when she'd entered the drawing room before dinner, and still, he found himself lost for words to describe just how very beautiful she was this evening.

"We agreed, and I accepted when I first found out who Her Highness was that there was no future between us. I cannot go back on my word now."

"Of course you can," Alessa said, clasping his arm and turning him to look at her. "And you will. My sister will not be happy, I think, unless you're beside her in life."

Drew scoffed, not believing that for a moment, even if the words sent hope through his blood. "She has done very well these past days without me. I have hardly seen her. We've barely talked two words since we arrived."

Alessa glanced over to her sister, a small smile lifting

her flawless lips. They certainly made the woman of this country beyond beautiful.

"No matter what is happening around you, Holly knows where you are. She watches you as much as you watch her. You may not think she is aware of your goings-on, but she is. Always. Do not ever underestimate her on that score. It would be to your detriment if you did."

Drew rubbed the back of his neck, glancing back toward Holly. Their gazes clashed. Held. Like a physical blow to the gut, he felt her interest. If she were his, he would go to her, stalk across this drawing room and lay claim to her before everyone present. Show all the nobility and royal guests that the future Queen of Atharia was an Englishman's lover, friend, and partner.

He sighed, wishing he could do such a thing.

"You will need to share Holly, should you wish to marry her. She has three great loves in her life. You, I believe, are one of them."

"And the others that I must share her with?" he asked, unsure he wanted to hear the answer to his question.

"Our homeland and its people. She will always do right by them, which means that sometimes you will have to accept she isn't always there for you. That she will miss important dates and milestones, but that will not mean that she loves you less. You will need to love her more to enable her to be queen without having to be concerned about your feelings when duty calls."

Drew frowned, staring down at the princess who was far more intelligent than he'd given her credit for. "Are you telling me, Princess Alessa not to sulk?"

She grinned up at him, and once again, he was shocked by the beauty of the woman. "I knew you were not a silly Englishman, my lord. I shall like having you as my brother. Now all you must do is not disappoint me and ensure it occurs. My sister deserves happiness, and I think that comes in the form of you." She poked him in the chest after her words, turned, and sauntered off.

He turned his attention back to where he'd seen Holly last and found her gone. Taller than most here, he looked over the heads of the guests but could not place her. Fear spiked in his gut, and he turned, searching behind him, only to see a flash of purple slip through the large terrace doors that opened to the outdoors. Without thought, he went after her, not to just ensure she was safe and no harm would come to her, but because he missed her voice, her touch, everything about the woman.

If only London could see him now. He shook his head at the thought. Oh, how they would laugh at Lord Balhannah and his falling hard for a woman. How they would laugh indeed.

*H*olly stepped out on the terrace, the warm night air enabling her to breathe. She took a couple of deep, calming breaths. The smell of salt, the sound of waves crashing on the cliffs, brought calm to her soul.

Drew was foremost in her mind, and his leaving. Everyone about her questioned his motives. Why he was with her at all and why he had not stayed in England. She had answered as best she could, but the one thing she did want to admit, could not say, was that he was here because she had wanted him to be by her side.

She could have demanded he stay in England, and Drew could not have stopped her, but she had not.

The sound of the terrace door behind her opening

pulled her from her thoughts, and she smiled the moment she recognized the light-haired and handsome Englishman she had fallen for. And she had fallen for him, utterly and completely. There was no use denying her feelings.

How she wanted to tell him all that she felt, how her body always yearned for his touch, how the sound of his voice made her heart stumble. How she never wanted him to go.

Drew came toward her, his steps slow and guarded. Was he unsure if he was welcome here? She went over to him, closing the space, and wrapped her arms about his waist, reveling in the sound of his heart beating against her ear. "I have missed you. Let us not spend so much time apart again. I need you beside me, Drew." More than she'd ever admitted.

He wrapped his arms about her, and she felt the light kiss he placed on her head. "I have missed you too. I saw you leave and wanted to make sure you are safe."

Holly leaned back in his arms, admiring her view of him. "I am well, just tired. Where are you staying? I asked for you to be in the room beside mine, but last evening when I knocked on that bedroom door, and I entered at no answer, I found it unoccupied."

He shrugged, pulling her close. "I'm at the opposite end of the house to your apartments. I think they are trying to tell me without words what they think of the English."

She frowned at the idea of Drew not feeling welcome here. He was her guest, and as such, he ought to be treated with respect, if not deference. "I shall speak to *Signore* Medici about this. I want you beside me, not kept from me."

"You want me that much?"

His words sent a thrill down her spine, and she moved closer, brushing her breasts against his chest. Drew felt good in her arms, and just as she had since the moment she'd met him, she wanted to wrap herself in his arms, feel him against her flesh, and never let go.

"I do want you so greatly." Holly leaned up, winding her arms about his neck, before kissing him. He took her lips, delving deep, and thrusting his tongue against hers. She moaned. Drew clasped her bottom and hoisted her against his erect manhood. Holly undulated against him, seeking release, anything to soothe the need that thrummed between her legs.

Somehow they forgot where they were or that they could be interrupted at any moment. The kiss turned frenzied, hard and fast, wet and delicious. Drew picked her up, hoisting her into his arms, and walked them to the end of the terrace. He set them on a stone seat, placing her on his lap. All the time, the kiss went on, mouths exploring and loving. Holly could not get enough. She clasped his hand, placing it on her leg, wanting him to touch her as he had before.

"Not here, Holly," he breathed against her mouth. "This isn't the place. No matter how much I want to assure you that if it were possible, I would take you over this chair."

She shuddered out a breath at the thought of such a thing. If she were never to marry this man or have a marriage of affection and love, passion, she would at least have this night—one night with the man she loved.

"Come to my room. Be with me?"

His eyes widened, and he pulled back, staring at her as if she had grown two heads. "What do you mean?"

Holly nodded, licking her lips, the need to taste him

again, to gain pleasure in his arms and desire she was unable to deny herself. No longer would she deny herself. "I want you, Drew, in all ways. I know it's a risk, but it is one that I'm willing to take." Holly slipped from his lap, leaning down one last time and kissing him gently. He stared at her, and she could see that he was debating her words, thinking, deciding.

"You know where I am when you're ready." Holly turned and left him then. A smile lifted her lips at the thought of him joining her, and he would, she was sure of it. He would not disappoint her, it was an impossibility for a man in love, and he loved her. Her sister had been correct on that score, and it was the only reason why she would give herself to him, heart and soul.

Tonight she would love a man who was not her husband, and the future Queen of Atharia would love every minute of it.

CHAPTER 19

*D*rew did not go to Holly's room as she had begged him. If he were to do one honorable thing in the world, other than bringing Holly back to Atharia and helping her regain her place as queen, he would also act the gentleman and not take her innocence.

She deserved better than a tumble with a man who was destined to return to England. To sleep with her lay madness, for them both. He would not be able to let her go, no matter what her thoughts were regarding marrying a man who was not of royal blood or had powerful people behind him.

He'd paced his room to the point that the Aubusson rug had a little indent at the end of his bed from his feet. The night gave way to dawn, and it was only when he could no longer keep awake that he succumbed to sleep, fully clothed and exhausted, mind and body, from having denied himself what was being given freely.

He woke several hours later to the sound of carriages leaving the estate and dragging himself from the bed. He glanced out the window to see Holly and her sister climbing up into a highly polished carriage before the drivers flicked the reins and the horses moved forward.

Drew bolted from the room, only to start at the sight of *Signore* Medici, who waited in the hallway outside his room. Did the man expect him to give chase, to stop Holly from leaving?

"Lord Balhannah, if you would refresh yourself and come downstairs, there is a carriage waiting for you. You're to return to the royal palace with Her Highness and Princess Alessa. Their uncle has had a seizure of some kind and has taken to his bed, unresponsive it would seem. The last thing this country needs is a war between the royal family members, and so perhaps God has shown a small mercy this day toward the crown princess to enable her to rule without obstruction."

Drew felt his mouth gape, and he swallowed, trying to think of what this would mean for them all. Holly would become queen, and he would have to leave. His decision of last night not to go to her room weighed on his shoulders. He'd made a mistake, for there would never now be another chance to be with her. With every roll of the carriage wheel, the farther it took her from him. The farther he was to having her in his arms.

Fuckkkk!

He turned back into his chamber, starting for his dressing room. "I shall be down in a few minutes. Just let me pack my things and freshen up."

"Of course, Lord Balhannah," *Signore* Medici said, his tone mocking.

Drew glanced at his lordship and did not miss the contempt the older gentleman had for him. He was not welcome here, it would seem, and with Holly traveling to the palace without him, perhaps he was no longer welcome with her as well.

*H*olly was aware of Drew within the party that traveled to the royal palace, and yet she did not seek him out or try to converse with him as she would have. Perhaps it was childish of her, immature and shallow, but anger still thrummed through her blood with his denial of her.

She had practically thrown herself at his head, and he'd declined the offer.

Heat touched her cheeks, and even now, two days after they had left the Medici estate, the mortification of his rejection still stung. Did he not find her attractive enough to sleep with? Did he not wish to lay with her because of who she was? Or was his plan all along to make her long for him so much that she'd throw all expectations aside and offer him marriage?

The idea that he'd played her this whole time simply to amuse himself took root and would not budge. She clenched her hands at her sides, anger thrumming through her veins as she climbed the large stairs in the foyer of her home, the palace they had grown up in. Alessa and she started toward Elena's suite of rooms, rejection biting at her silk slippers.

They made the private part of the palace closed for their own personal use and turned toward Elena's room. Her sister, having expected them it would seem and was listening out, glanced down the passage. Seeing them, she ran from her room, pulling them both into an immovable hug.

"Holly! Alessa, I'm so glad that you're here," Elena cried, not willing to let them go.

Holly hugged her back, hating the thought of what she'd been put through these past months. "We're here, dearest, and all will be well. Have they told you of Uncle's condition?"

Elena shook her dark curls, her face pensive. "No, nothing. Only that he fell ill while entertaining and has not been able to be roused since. It has now been five days."

Holly started toward her room, taking her sisters' arms and pulling them along with her. "I shall go and see my uncle soon. My secretary here in the palace has been informed to start preparations for my coronation. I'm one and twenty next week, and so there will be no impediment to my taking the crown."

"What if Uncle wakes up?" Elena asked, closing the door to Holly's room and locking it. "He has been the worst of men. I have been locked up for months." Elena turned to Alessa. "I'm so very glad you escaped and were unharmed. I worried about you. Uncle said that you had not escaped, but had also not been seen. He let me believe the worst had happened."

Holly shook her head. The man was the worst of his kind. He would burn in hell for all that he'd done to their family and his homeland. "He can no longer hurt us."

"There are people here who do not want you on the throne. People who are loyal to him, for reasons that are unfathomable to me," Elena said.

"I need to know who they are. If you would make a list for me, I shall deal with them as soon as may be. I will not have trouble here. Our people and our own lives deserve better than that."

"I agree," both her sisters said in unison.

Holly stood, needing to go see her uncle and confirm for herself that he was as she had been told. That this was not yet another plan of foolery on his part.

"I shall return soon. There is business that I must attend." Holly walked to the door before turning back. "Lock the door on my departure, just to be safe."

Her uncle's suite was not far, rooms that used to be her father's, and by right should be hers at this very moment. The large, opulent space was guarded by two of her former guards at the door. They bowed at her presence, opening the door without word or opposition.

Holly entered the room, and dread coiled in her stomach at what she found. All her father's things that made the space special, an honorable suite of rooms fit for a king, were gone. In their place was nothing at all, stark and bland, the vibrant potted plants and paintings from the masters of the world gone. All that was left was the gold that adorned a lot of the furniture, making the room look gaudy and cheap, even if it was far from being so.

She went to the bedroom and entered, stopping at the sight of her uncle in his bed. Small and frail, he did not appear to be the same man whom she'd left here only several months before. His face was gaunt, his hair almost white and thinning on top. To her, he looked ill and as if he had been so for quite some time.

No movement came from the bed, and his chest barely rose, his breathing shallow. Holly dismissed the two footmen who stood beside the wall, in wait or waiting for direction. "Leave us," she commanded, waiting for the two servants to close the door.

Holly sat on a chair beside the bed and glared at the man who had tried to take her life. Twice, in fact. Her gaze flicked to the pillows behind his head, and for the first time in her life, she considered using one to snuff out her uncle. No one would know if she did the act, and no one would question her being the crown princess.

She slumped back in the chair, watching her uncle's chest, feeling nothing but contempt for the man. She did not pray for his soul, merely waited and watched as he took his final breaths, and when he did, she did not kiss him goodbye, but turned her back and left. His reign was over, and now hers was about to begin.

CHAPTER 20

A week later, the celebrations for the crown princess's twenty-first birthday were in full swing. Hundreds of people had come from all around Atharia to see her take her place as future monarch with the coronation happening tomorrow.

Drew stood at the side of the ballroom, Princess Alessa by his side as he watched Holly dance the waltz with Prince Gustov of Greece. Drew had decided that after Holly's coronation tomorrow, he would leave Atharia and never look back.

Over the last week since her uncle's passing, there had been no contact between them. He'd sat in his room, waiting for as long as he could for her to seek him out. He'd walked the gardens and met as many of the staff and guests here at the palace that he could to bide the time. He knew most people present now by their first names.

No more would he wait around like a fool waiting for a crumb of notice. He was no one's fool, and he would not, no matter how much he adored Holly, be hers either. She did not want him here, and so he would leave.

Drew swallowed the lump in his throat at the idea of leaving her, but he'd come here to see her rightfully take her place, and she had done all that she promised to do. She had returned to her country, and by the grace of God, had not had to fight her uncle in a war the country could not afford.

She was happy and settled back in the palace and had ample suitable royal-blooded men fawning at her golden skirts each day. She did not need him here.

Like a physical blow to the gut, he watched Prince Gustov leaned down to say something that amused Her Highness. The crowd that circled them danced around them, laughed, and admired the striking pair.

Drew hated the bastard with the loathing of a thousand men.

He turned from the vision they made and strode from the room, not bothering to excuse himself from Princess Alessa, who called after him. He blindly walked up a deserted passage that ran alongside the ballroom, the muffled sound of the waltz baiting him at his mistake, of why she had pushed him away.

He had denied her what she wanted. Him. And now she would deny him the very same.

A door along the passage lay open, the room abandoned and dark. Perfect. He went in and slumped down on the silk lounge that sat before an unlit fire. Muffled laughter and music echoed through the palace, and Drew shook his head, unable to comprehend how he was here and how he had lost her affection.

For a woman who seemed fond of him, affectionate and kind, she certainly knew how to stick him with a sword well enough through the heart.

He lay his head back on the lounge, staring at the ceiling. He looked to the side and spied a decanter of brandy. Leaning over, he clasped the crystal jug and drank deep, forgoing a glass.

If tonight was his last night in Atharia with Holly and he was to be alone, what better way to go than to drink himself into oblivion until the pain that coursed through every fiber of his soul numbed and dissipated.

"Lord Balhannah, how very far away you are from London. I did not expect to find you here, but was rightfully pleased to have it confirmed tonight at the ball."

Drew started, sitting up at the sight of Lady Ambrose, Earl Courtenay's widow, and heaven help him, one of his former lovers.

"You look lost, Drew darling. Is everything well?"

Unable to fathom that she was here, he ran a hand over his face, clearing his vision. He'd never been able to deny himself her body when she offered it, but the thought of touching her now left him wanting to cast up his accounts. "Leave me, Josephine. I'm not good company to keep."

She ignored his request, coming to sit beside him on the lounge, her body hard up against his side, one arm laying gently atop his thigh. "I can make you good company, Drew. Shall we have a little fun abroad while we're here?" The woman slipped her tongue along her top lip and damn it, his cock twitched in his breeches.

He took another long pull of his brandy, the room spinning. "No. You need to leave. I want to be alone."

"You're not pining for the Crown Princess, are you?" She clicked her tongue, shaking her head, her long, blonde curls bouncing about her neck. "I saw you watching her like a pining little puppy. You must remember, the princess will be crowned queen tomorrow. We may be nobility,

Drew but even our stature will only get you so far. She is not for you."

He frowned, hating her words and the truth of them that rung like a bell in his head. "I know that." Not that the fact made the situation any more palatable. Nothing would make leaving Holly so.

She ran her hand along his jaw, tipping his face toward her. "I can make you feel better, Drew. We've done it before. It is not like we're not acquainted. Let us both find pleasure tonight." Her hand slipped over his waistcoat toward his breeches. He caught her fingers just before they reached his front falls. "No, Josephine."

"Come now." She chuckled, and before he could stop her, she had straddled his legs, thrusting herself against his cock. He stared up at her, feeling oddly numb, no matter how much she tried to arouse him. "You know you will enjoy it, Drew. You've never complained before."

For a moment, he debated with himself what to do. Allow her to take him, try to fuck his pain away. He sighed, knowing it was no use. Nothing but Holly could do that. He clasped her hips, and she half-sighed, half-moaned at his touch. He was sorry to disappoint her, but tonight there was only one woman he wanted, and it was not the one that occupied his lap, but the one that occupied his heart.

*H*olly had seen Drew flee the ballroom and, after the waltz, had set off to find him. She was ashamed of herself for treating him the way she had. Pushing him away as if he had meant nothing at all to her. He meant everything, in fact.

She loved him, and tomorrow, she would tell her people and her family of her choice once she was queen.

That it would not be a prince of royal birth, but an Englishman. One who had saved her life and her happiness. A future duke who held her heart in his hand, no matter if over the last week, she had tried so very hard to shift his hold on her.

The sound of a woman's moan caught her attention, and Holly hastened her steps. Was someone injured or being threatened in some way? Glancing into a darkened, unoccupied room, she gasped at the sight of Drew and the widow Courtenay in an indelicate position.

Anger thrummed through her, hot and wild. How dare he!

Holly stepped into the room, ordering the two guards who followed her to light the candles. Lady Courtenay had the wit to remove herself from Lord Balhannah's lap, As for Drew, he slumped back on the settee, his reaction guarded, shuttered in fact.

"Get out and remove yourself from the palace," she commanded, not sparing her ladyship another look. The woman fled the room without a word. "Please leave us," she commanded her guards as they too walked from the room, closing the door behind them.

Drew gestured toward her, his eyes unfocused and glassy. "Ah, so you have demeaned yourself to come see me, Your Highness. How privileged I am by your company."

His words stung, and she understood why. She had kept him from her, had not allowed him to gain an audience, even though her sisters had told her to stop being so obstinate. Stop punishing him. It was Drew's fault that she was so very mad with him. If he had only come to her room, finished what they had started on the terrace at the Medici estate, all would be well between them. She could not understand why he'd denied her. There was only one reason in her mind she could think of. He had not wanted her. She had not captured his heart as she hoped she had.

"You seemed very well pleased with how I found you tonight, my lord. Do not act the injured party now."

He cocked his brow, twisting his head a little to look up at her. "Oh, I am the injured party. You have ignored me this past week, and why? Because I did not tumble you to your bed and fuck you like a whore."

Holly swallowed, clamping her jaw as she fought to control her rioting emotions. "I thought that was what you wanted from me. It was what I wanted from you, but less baseless as you've described it. And yet here you are, caught in a darkened room with one of my guests. I guess you really were a libertine in London and now Atharia as well. How proud you must be."

He scoffed, stood, and came to tower over her. "You're as cruel as your uncle. After everything that had occurred between us, how could you throw me aside as you did?"

"You threw me aside first, my lord. I was merely leveling the score."

Drew gaped at her, running a hand through his already mussed hair. The sight of him, being this close, reminded her of why she longed for him. She did not want to hurt him. She loved him.

"I did not want you to regret your choice of being with me. Of all the times that I've been with a woman, I have never deflowered a virgin. If I had, I would have married her. I could not marry you. I'm not good enough for the Atharia crown, or its people."

His words cut like a knife, and she blinked away the tears that welled in her eyes. He was good enough for both herself and her people. It was her fault she had allowed him to think otherwise, made him agree to see their friendship and false marriage as a temporary fix, not a long-term possibility.

"And so you're looking for another tupp, and here I find you in an indelicate position with a woman. How fickle you men are when you do not get what you want from one person, you merely find it with another."

"Be assured, madam that had you walked in on me fucking Lady Courtenay, you would be under no question as to what I was doing. As it was, she stood, did she not, and both of us were perfectly attired. I was not fucking her. I wasn't doing anything with her but telling her to leave."

Holly pushed past him, having heard enough. He clasped her arm and wrenched her to his chest. "I refused her offer. I do not want to fuck Lady Courtenay or anyone else. I want you, damn it. The one woman whom I cannot have and whom from her actions over the last week does not want me either."

His deep, gravelly words coiled pleasure through her core, and her body ached and burned for his touch. Even after walking in on him with another woman, still, she craved his touch, wanting his bruising kisses and devastating desire.

She stared at him, her mind on a tightrope and threatening to tip either way. Toward or away from Drew. His eyes darkened with need, and he made a choice for her. He seized her lips, kissing her with punishing force. The desire that thrummed from Drew, his trembling hands as they clasped her face, his frenzied kiss ought to scare her, but it did not. Nothing he ever did would ever scare her. She loved every moment of being in his arms.

Holly clasped his face and kissed him back. He pulled away, silent questions in his eyes.

Want me. Pick me.

She seized his lips again and let herself fall his way, into his arms and where she believed she always should have been.

*D*rew's legs threatened to buckle under the need that coursed through him. Having Holly back in his arms was an elixir that would forever give him strength and purpose. He seized her mouth, laid claim to her soft lips. Their tongues tangled, soft moans intertwined with hungry growls.

He slipped his arms beneath her ass and hoisted her onto his waist. She wrapped her legs about him, kissing him. Her hair tumbled down around her shoulders, pins scattered. Drew tore at the back of her dress, needing it off, to see her. He stepped toward a daybed in the corner of the room, wanting Holly beneath him, moaning and arching as he made her come.

"Tell me you want me. Tell me this is not something you will regret come morning."

She worked his cravat, ripping it free from his neck and throwing it to the floor. Her eyes met his, and he read the desire burning in her green orbs. His gut clenched at her beauty, at her willingness to be with him. She was far superior to him. He did not deserve such a gift.

"I will never regret you, Drew." Her gaze dipped to his lips before she kissed him again.

His control snapped, and he tumbled them to the bed. Holly chuckled but Drew burned with a need that would not abate. This was too fast. He needed to slow down, take his time. Holly rubbed against him, her knees lifting and bringing her core to hit against his cock. All thought dissipated and Drew ripped at his front falls, freeing his cock that strained with need.

Her hands slid over his back before she reached around and clasped his member. He clamped his eyes shut and saw stars. Her touch, the slip of her fingers strong about his member, made it almost impossible not to spend in her hand. Drew thrust into her hold, and she purred, sending his wits to spiral.

It was his turn to tease, to watch her enjoy his touch. Drew leaned back, breaking her hold, and hoisted her dress up about her waist. Her cunny glistened, aroused and wet. He slipped a hand over her folds, rubbing the pad of his thumb across her clit. She mewled and undulated beneath his touch. He licked his fingers, tasting her, earthy and sweet. With a slowness that he did not think himself capable of right at this time, he pressed his fingers into her. Pushing into her tight, wet heat.

So fucking hot.

"Drew," she moaned, her muscles clamping around his fingers and giving him a taste of what he would relish very soon.

He fucked her with his hand, reached down, and forced her to watch him when she closed her eyes, her head thrashing from side to side. "Look at me," he demanded, his cock oozing pre-cum as she climbed her way to release.

Just when he could feel her at her highest ebb, he pulled out, replacing his fingers with his tongue. She gasped, her hands reaching for his head. He thought she would push him away, but she did not. Her grip on his hair tightened, urged him to remain where he was.

He lapped at her cunny, kissing and teasing her engorged nubbin until she was riding his face, taking her pleasure, taking all that she wanted from him. Drew stroked his way down to her core, fucking her with his tongue, teasing her clit with his thumb. He would never get enough of her. From this day forward, he wanted to wake up with her gasping his name as he took her, made love to her.

He taunted between her folds and suckled on her clit, flicking it with his tongue. She came hard, his name a repeated chant filling the room. He did not stop his assault until she was spent, her legs falling open, her arms flat out on the bed.

Drew came over her, placing himself at her core. Her hooded, opaque eyes opened, watching him before she reached up, clasped the front of his shirt, and pulled him down. He kissed her deep and thrust into her heat. They moaned, and Drew doubted he had ever felt more alive, more in need of anyone in his life.

"Ah, Holly," he gasped, thrusting deeper, faster.

She did not shy away from him, but wrapped her legs about his waist and lifted her hips, taking him deeper, moving beneath him to take her own pleasure and control.

His breath hitched, his thrusts increased. The muffled sound of their moans mingled through their kiss, the slap of skin on skin a symphony he'd never forget.

"Oh, Drew, do not stop. That feels so good."

He wouldn't stop. Nothing, not even Holly's entire army, could pull him away from tupping her right at this moment. They were like a beast with two backs, frenzied and without heed. His balls tightened, and an ache filled his lower gut. He was close.

He fought not to spend, wanting her to climax a second time. Biting down on his desire, his wish was granted, not a few moments later.

She wrenched up, his name a muffled scream against his chest. Her core muscles flexed and tightened, and it was too much. No matter how well-versed in the act of love-making, no man could deny that call to pleasure.

He let go of his control and came, fucked with deep, hard thrusts as he let himself go. The pleasure was shocking in its capacity to make him senseless. Never had he ever come so hard. Enjoyed himself so much, or wanted to do the same thing again and again for the rest of his life.

Drew flopped down beside her on the daybed, pulling her into the crook of his arm. He glanced down at her and found a self-satisfied grin on her lips that made him chuckle. "Did I live up to your expectations, my love?" he asked, not caring that he'd used an endearment he had yet to voice out loud.

She purred, wrapping her leg over his waist and her arm over his stomach, idly playing with his bellybutton. "More than lived up to them." She glanced up at him, a wicked light in her eyes. "I am wondering when we can do this all again. Had I known being with a man could be so enjoyable, I would have married at my first opportunity."

The mention of marriage, and hers in particular, sent panic to race through his blood. His stomach churned. "Not all men are created equal. You may have married a dud. Perhaps you ought to marry me instead just to be secure in your choice of a bed partner."

She raised her brow, her eyes wide. "Did you just ask me to marry you, Lord Balhannah?"

He reached over, pushing a lock of her hair from her face, giving him a clearer view of her beauty that took his breath away every time he saw it. "If I said yes, would you consider me?" He was taking a risk. He knew they had agreed that they were only ever meant to pretend, that he wasn't equal to her status. That she would marry a prince or no one at all, but he could not help himself. The heart wanted what the heart wanted, and his organ beat for the woman in his arms and no one else.

"If it were my choice, you know I would choose you, Drew." She frowned, her eyes growing sad. "Please do not make this parting between us any harder than it already is."

He stilled at her words and the finality of them. Even after all that they shared, having made love to her, being in love with her, and she would still turn him away? Drew sat up, climbing off the daybed, righting his clothing as best he could. He kept his view of her at bay, did not need to see the disheveled, well-bedded woman whom he loved and adored.

Not that he could disrespect her for her choice. A queen to her people to the very end, she was only doing what she thought was right for her homeland. She would forgo the desire of her own heart to keep her people safe and protected. Marriage to another royal family would ensure that. Drew could not hate her for such a sacrifice, even if the idea of leaving her tore him in two.

Dressed, he strode to the door, halting, but unable to look at her. "I wish you well in all that you do in life, Holly. I wish you happiness and no more pain. You will be queen from tomorrow. You no longer need me here. I shall return to England on the high tide tomorrow evening. Goodbye."

Drew walked from the room, shutting the door quietly behind him. His vision blurred as he strode into the depths of the palace. Away from the ball and away from Holly. He would leave the court tonight. He could not stay here. There was nothing left for him here now.

CHAPTER 21

*H*olly stepped out onto the palace's balcony and waved to her people, thanking them for their support on this triumphant day. Her sisters stood beside her, waving and smiling, happy that the crown was back in their control and that the people would no longer suffer under the tyrannical rule of their uncle.

The afternoon waned, and Holly's attention shifted to the port that she could just make out through the houses that sat beyond the royal square. A large ship's mask peeked up above the roofline of Atharia's homes, and her heart stuttered in her chest.

Drew would be on that ship this evening. Sailing away to England and from her, and why? Because she'd not stopped him when he'd stated he would go. Because she had not said yes, even though her heart screamed at the joy of his proposal.

With one last wave to the crowd, she turned, ready to face her court and announce her future and that of the palace. She entered the throne room, stepped up on the raised dais, and sat in her throne. A dark-blue canopy hung above her, gilded edging and a carpet made of the same pattern beneath her feet.

The room quieted, and Holly took a calming breath, ready to declare her rules. She spoke of the suffering of her people, how she would combat hunger and homelessness. Her plans for schools. For all children to be free of child labor. The supplement she would enact for parents to keep their children in school instead of pulling them out to work in the mines and fields.

She spoke of making the port deeper, increasing imports and exports. Her hope that soon Atharia would be looked upon as a powerful nation, self-reliant but open to trade with other countries. A fair democracy governed by a government and not the royal family, although they would be there to guide and assist when needed.

Gasps sounded at her declaration, but it was no different from what other countries had done and had prospered from. A rich, ruling family whom the people could not choose to be their voice was not modern thinking. She wanted her people to be able to choose whom they believed was in line with their views. The royal family of Atharia would never again place the people in such jeopardy as her uncle had done. She would not allow it, and she would make it law that it was so.

"On the matter of my future happiness, and the king consort who shall be by my side, I wish to inform you that I have made my choice and my choice is final. A forthcoming offer will be made to the Marquess of Balhannah, future Duke Sotherton of England, to be my husband. My choice is final and will not be debated." Her eyes met those of her private secretary, his eyes bulging out of his head along with everyone else's. Her sisters, however, smiled with happiness that told Holly she had chosen wisely. She had picked the man she loved, and there would never be an error with such a choice. "That is all."

Holly stood, walking from the room, her sisters and ladies in waiting following close on her heels. Muffled gasps and chatter sounded behind her, and she raised her chin, not caring a bit for their opinions. A weight that had plagued her for weeks lifted from her shoulders, and for the first time in an age, she felt as though she could breathe.

She turned to her secretary. "I need to travel to the wharf right away."

"Yes, Your Majesty," he said, striding past her and yelling out orders for the royal carriage to be prepared for the queen.

"Your Majesty, may I speak to you?"

Holly turned at the sound of Niccolo's voice. "Leave us a moment," she said to her ladies and sisters who surrounded her. "What is it, Niccolo?" she asked, not willing to hear any more prejudice against Drew.

Her guard stood with his hands behind his back, head bowed. "I stand before you and offer you my humble apologies and hope that you will grant me the honor to remain by your side as your humble servant and protector."

She narrowed her eyes, hoping she could trust him. The last few weeks had been fraught with tension. It was no secret Niccolo did not like Drew, but he could not remain here if that were still the case. "I lost faith in you, Niccolo. You acted out of character and above your position. Why?"

A pained looked crossed his features. "I distrusted Lord Balhannah that is true, but I have come to accept he is an honorable man. A man you can trust, and who is dependable with secrets the Crown keeps. I was wrong, Your

Highness. I saw shadows and threats where perhaps there were none. Know that if you allow me to serve you, that I shall support and keep you and your family safe for the remainder of my days."

Niccolo's words were what Holly wanted to hear, and she was proud of the stoic, sometimes too opinionated guard that he had apologized. It would not have been easy for him. She smiled, reaching out to pat his shoulder. "Thank you for telling me this, Niccolo. I will admit to fearing a time or two that you worked for my uncle."

Niccolo gasped, horror written across his features. "Never, Your Highness."

She smiled, satisfied at the sincerity she heard in his voice. "I know that now, and I'm pleased you sought me out to explain. Of course you may remain in your post. Our family will be safer for it."

"Thank you, Your Majesty," he said, bowing and step-ping back.

Holly turned toward her sisters, unable to remove the smile from her face. "Now, I'm off to win my future husband. Do you approve my choice?" she asked, meeting both her sisters' gazes.

Alessa hugged her, and Elena joined them. "Oh, Holly, I endorse your choice one hundred percent. Lord Balhannah is the most honorable, sweet man. You will not regret your choice," Alessa said.

"I think he's dashing," Elena returned, her eyes misting with tears. "I would love a husband to look upon me as he does you. Anyone who has seen you together knows he adores you so. I'm so thrilled with your choice."

Tears welled in Holly's eyes, and she sniffed, blinking away the tears. "Thank you, my dearest hearts. I can only hope that he will forgive me for not declaring my hand last evening."

"He will understand, once you explain," Alessa said, turning Holly toward the corridor she needed to walk down to make her way downstairs and to the carriage. "Now go. We look forward to your return."

Holly started down the passage, increasing her pace until she was running. Not very queeny, but then, what was that when there was a husband to catch before the evening tide? One must run when running is required. She would make that rule law as well if she had to.

*D*rew stood at the ship's bow, staring out over the vast ocean they would soon be sailing on. He did not want to leave, remove himself from Holly. The severing that tore his soul in two threatened to keelhaul him.

He adored her, but he had asked for her hand, and she had said no. In fact, she had said nothing at all, which he wasn't sure was worse.

A commotion behind him sounded, and he turned. A shining black carriage with the royal standard flag waved on its roof—a bevy of armed men standing guard both in front, behind, and at the side of the carriage. A woman descended the steps, her golden gown, a crown atop her head, made his breath hitch.

Holly. Queen of Atharia.

He did not move, scared that if he did, it might shift some fantasy he was seeing before him and dissipate into the salty sea breeze.

She strolled along the docks toward him, taking the time to talk to the people who gathered to meet her. Her smile warmed his heart, her care of these people as genuine as ever he'd known her to be.

Her guards did not try to stop her from speaking to her people, and already he could see the type of queen she would be. Present and calm, a kind and caring queen that all countries needed.

Her gaze lifted toward his ship, and over the many people separating them, and he knew she had spotted him. Saying something quickly to her people, she moved on, her determination not to be delayed evident with each step. And before he could gain his wits, she was before him, looking up at him with what he hoped was optimism in her green eyes.

"Lord Balhannah," she said, and nothing else.

He cleared his throat of the lump that had formed there. "Your Majesty," he replied. His eyes devoured every morsel of her. She looked stunningly beautiful, young, and strong. He was in awe of her, and he swallowed again, fearful that he would break down and beg her to not let him go. He could only dream of such a thing.

"I have come here today, as the Queen of Atharia to ask you, now that I'm at liberty to do so, for you to be my husband, my lover, my best friend, and king consort, if you will have me."

Drew stilled at her question, unable to comprehend for a moment what she was asking. Had she really just asked him to marry her? Hope eviscerated the despair of only minutes before, and he pulled her against him, holding her so tight that he doubted even her guards could come between them right at that moment.

"Do you mean it?" he gasped against her neck. "Truly, do you wish for me to be your husband, Holly?"

She pulled back a little, meeting his eyes. "I do. I could

not say yes yesterday, no matter how much I had wanted to. But today, as queen, I may choose whomever I want, and no one can naysay me. You are my equal, in all ways that matter. I love you. I think I may have loved you the moment you shoved me down in that sandy hole and saved my life."

He laughed even though his vision of Holly was decidedly blurry. "Yes, my darling, beautiful, kind friend. I shall marry you, support you, be there for you and your people. I adore you, my love, and I love you. I think I may have loved you from the moment you slapped my face on the beach to ensure my survival."

Holly laughed, wrapping her arms about his neck, kissing him before all who were behind them. Cheers reigned loud on the dock, people hollered with laughter and cries of congratulations. Drew deepened the kiss, forgoing protocol and etiquette for the moment and simply enjoyed having her in his arms. He would marry her, and they would love each other until the end of days.

He would be her king consort and anything else she demanded. He was hers to rule, both in love and country.

EPILOGUE

Three months later, Sotherton, England

$\mathcal{H}$olly stood beside Drew in the Sotherton library, the Duke of Sotherton staring at them as if they had both lost their minds. "You're the Queen of Atharia all this time? My son," the duke said, pointing toward Drew with an accusatory finger, "helped you escape an attack from your uncle, and then you married him?"

Drew chuckled, and Holly smiled at the older gentleman's incapacity to accept what they had just told him. They had not written, preferring to travel back to England and tell His Grace to his face of his only son's marriage, to introduce him to his new daughter-in-law as who she truly was.

His Grace was beyond pleased the first time they feigned marriage, but to hear the full truth seemed to have shocked him to a disturbing gray color that did not look healthy.

"Your Grace," Holly said, going around the desk,

clasping his hand. "I know this is a shock. We have lied to you, yes, but it was only ever for your own safety. I love your son, and he loves me, but his being my husband will mean that the majority of his time will be abroad. I hope you're not disappointed."

His Grace stared up at her, blinking. "While I shall miss our verbal bouts, my boy, I am happy for you." The duke stood, going around the desk and wrapping his son in his arms. Drew smiled at Holly over his father's shoulder, and her heart rejoiced at the sight.

"I shall come home as much as I can, and I hope that you, too, will come to visit me. We promise to look after you, Father."

The older man pulled back, tears welling in his aged eyes. "I would cherish to visit with you and in time, my grandchildren."

Holly grinned, rubbing a hand over her stomach that was not the least bit bulged, but in any case, carried the little bundle of love that she and Drew had made. "That is what else we wished to tell you, Your Grace. You're going to be a grandfather, so I suppose you shall have to come to visit in about six months."

The duke stumbled back, and Drew reached for him, steadying his feet. "You're *enceinte*?"

"We are, Father," Drew said, pride filling his handsome visage. Butterflies took flight in Holly's stomach, and she marveled at the thought that he made her breath catch still. She hoped that it would never change and forever be perfect, and just as it was now.

"I do not know what to say," the duke hollered, clasping his son and lifting him off the ground, before hugging Holly in a more orderly fashion. "I'm going to be a grandfather. Oh, I do so hope it will be a boy, two boys, in fact, one who will take over Atharia and one who may take over the dukedom here, if the elder child agrees. How wonderful," the duke sighed, wiping his eyes with the handkerchief he fumbled out of his pocket.

"I'm sure we shall work something out that is suitable for all our children, Father."

Holly joined Drew, wrapping her arm about his waist. "There is one more thing we would ask you, Your Grace?" Holly said, glancing up at her husband, who stared down at her with the most adorable, pleasing look.

"Of course, anything at all," the duke said, sitting back down at his desk and smiling up at them.

"We ask if you would be willing to sponsor my sister to a Season in London next year. She had been kept a prisoner by my uncle in Atharia, and I wish for her to enjoy herself a little before she settles and marries like I have. My youngest sister is not yet old enough to travel abroad, but Princess Alessa is. Perhaps Drew's Aunt Rosemary may suit as a chaperone. She will have guards, all who are trained not to cause a stir, but I feel I owe it to her. Alessa has the kindest soul, she will not be a bother, I promise you."

The duke stared at them both a moment before he stood. "It would be an honor to have Princess Alessa stay as my guest. Aunt Rosemary will be more than accommodating, and I shall have her move into the ducal London home for the Season's duration. We shall have a jolly good time, and I'm sure the princess will return home a very enlightened lady."

Not too enlightened, Holly hoped, but it was what best for Alessa. She had been down a little of late. She needed laughter and gaiety in her life, and London could give her that before she married. Perhaps even she too would find herself an Englishman to love.

"It is settled then. You are for London next Season. Alessa will return with you to England after you come to visit for the birth of our child," Holly said, pleased with the turn of today's events.

"That is a royal proposition that I cannot refuse," the duke declared, standing once more. "This calls for a toast. I shall ring for champagne."

The duke rang for a servant and Drew turned to her, wrapping his arms about her back, pulling her close. "You're a good sister and wonderful wife. How is it that I've been fortunate to win your love?"

Holly wrapped her arms around his neck, kissing him and not caring they had an audience. "Because I love you just as much, and because of one other small detail."

Drew frowned down at her, confused. "Oh, really, and what was that?"

Holly played with Drew's hair at the back of his nape, knowing how much he enjoyed her touch there. "Because I asked you to marry me and you said yes."

"Ahhh, yes, of course." He pulled her close, rocking her in his arms. "I do believe I asked you first, however, so it would seem that I am the victor in that bout."

"Perhaps." She shrugged. "But I think that in this marriage we are both the winners in the end. I'm truly blessed, I know that I was born into greatness, but I now know what it is like to truly love and be happy. I adore you so much, Drew. Promise me that we'll always be there for each other, no matter what occurs."

He kissed her soundly. "Always, my love and forever, my queen."

Dear Reader,

Thank you for taking the time to read *To Dream of You*! I hope you enjoyed the first book in my new, The Royal House of Atharia series.

I adore my readers, and I'm so thankful for your support. If you're able, I would appreciate an honest review of *To Dream of You*. As they say, feed an author, leave a review!

If you'd like to continue with, The Royal House of Atharia series, *A Royal Proposition* will be available in 2021. You can pre-order your copy today!

Tamara Gill

A ROYAL PROPOSITION

THE ROYAL HOUSE OF ATHARIA, BOOK 2

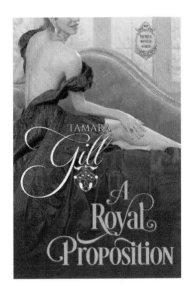

Coming 2021 - Pre-order your copy today!

LORDS OF LONDON SERIES
AVAILABLE NOW!

Dive into these charming historical romances! In this six-book series, Darcy seduces a virginal duke, Cecilia's world collides with a roguish marquess, Katherine strikes a deal with an unlucky earl and Lizzy sets out to conquer a very wicked Viscount. These stories plus more adventures in the Lords of London series! Available now through Amazon or read free with KindleUnlimited.

KISS THE WALLFLOWER SERIES AVAILABLE NOW!

If the roguish Lords of London are not for you and wall-flowers are more your cup of tea, this is the series for you. My Kiss the Wallflower series, are linked through friendship and family in this four-book series. You can grab a copy on Amazon or read free through KindleUnlimited.

TO MADDEN A MARQUESS

TO TEMPT AN EARL

TO VEX A VISCOUNT

TO DARE A DUCHESS

TO MARRY A MARCHIONESS

LORDS OF LONDON - BOOKS 1-3 BUNDLE

LORDS OF LONDON - BOOKS 4-6 BUNDLE

To Marry a Rogue Series

ONLY AN EARL WILL DO

ONLY A DUKE WILL DO

ONLY A VISCOUNT WILL DO

ONLY A MARQUESS WILL DO

ONLY A LADY WILL DO

A Time Traveler's Highland Love Series

TO CONQUER A SCOT

TO SAVE A SAVAGE SCOT

TO WIN A HIGHLAND SCOT

Time Travel Romance

DEFIANT SURRENDER

A STOLEN SEASON

Scandalous London Series

A GENTLEMAN'S PROMISE

A CAPTAIN'S ORDER

A MARRIAGE MADE IN MAYFAIR

SCANDALOUS LONDON - BOOKS 1-3 BUNDLE

High Seas & High Stakes Series

HIS LADY SMUGGLER

HER GENTLEMAN PIRATE

HIGH SEAS & HIGH STAKES - BOOKS 1-2 BUNDLE

Daughters Of The Gods Series

BANISHED-GUARDIAN-FALLEN

DAUGHTERS OF THE GODS - BOOKS 1-3 BUNDLE

Stand Alone Books

TO SIN WITH SCANDAL

OUTLAWS

ABOUT THE AUTHOR

Tamara is an Australian author who grew up in an old mining town in country South Australia, where her love of history was founded. So much so, she made her darling husband travel to the UK for their honeymoon, where she dragged him from one historical monument and castle to another.

A mother of three, her two little gentlemen in the making, a future lady (she hopes) and a part-time job keep her busy in the real world, but whenever she gets a moment's peace she loves to write romance novels in an array of genres, including regency, medieval and time travel.

www.tamaragill.com
tamaragillauthor@gmail.com

Manufactured by Amazon.ca
Bolton, ON